DAY IN, DAY OUT

HÉCTOR AGUILAR CAMÍN

TRANSLATION BY CHANDLER THOMPSON

schaffner
press

Tucson, Arizona

First English Language Edition
Trade Paperback Original
License to reprint granted by Guillermo
Schavelzon Agencia Literaria
Tel (34) 932 011 310 * Fax (34) 932 003 886 *
info@schavelzon.com

Cover Design: Dan Stiles
Interior Design: Darci Slaten

ISBN: 978-1-943156-26-9 (Paperback)
ISBN: 978-1-943156-27-6 (PDF)
ISBN: 978-1-943156-28-3 (EPub)
ISBN: 978-1-943156-29-0 (Mobipocket)

For Library of Congress Cataloguing-
in-Publication Information,
Contact the Publisher

Printed in the United States

DAY IN, DAY OUT

HÉCTOR AGUILAR CAMÍN

TRANSLATION BY CHANDLER THOMPSON

"This ambitious novel memorably brings together recent history, horrific crimes, and an ever-present sense of corruption."

~*Kirkus Reviews*

"I wish 'Speaking of Mysteries' was posting [an] interview with Héctor Aguilar Camín, but I don't speak Spanish. After reading this book, though, I was sorely tempted to learn. I'm taking Spanish lessons in anticipation of Aguilar Camín's next book."

~Nancie Clare, former editor of *LA Times Magazine* and author of *The Spirit of Beverly Hills*

"*Death in Veracruz*, the first novel by Mexican author Héctor Aguilar Camín to be translated into English, [is]…at its heart, the noir romance of one man's unquenched passion for an old college friend's wife."

~Tom Nolan, *The Wall Street Journal*

"The narrative depends on a complex political context, and it is a tribute to Aguilar Camín's gripping style that he can describe the machinations of government without lapsing into dry exposition."

~Charlotte Whittle, *Reading In Translation*

IDON'T KNOW WHY I'M GOING to Olivares's wake. He's not my friend, and I don't know his family. *Felo* Fernández tells me the wake is tomorrow. He says, "Maybe we'll run into each other." I have a soft spot for *Felo* Fernández. I haven't seen him in years, and much of what I hear about him strains credibility. That he chews glass when he's drunk, for example. Or that he's ridden an elephant. He once hired an elephant so a politician running for office could ride it into a town. The candidate wants to let everyone know times have changed and he stands for change. There's a circus camped on the edge of the town; *Felo* thinks riding into town on an elephant is a great way for the candidate to get his message across. The stunt is a resounding success, but, like tasters who must try their masters' food, *Felo* has to ride the elephant first.

Olivares's friends are all at the wake.

I don't know if friendship is the right word for what brings these people together. They're classmates who later became Olivares's cronies in the political science department of the old national university. Closing my eyes, I can still see the small school of old with its patch of lawn and its cafeteria full of the beautiful girls he lusted after first as a student, then as a professor, and finally as department head.

The best and brightest of the Olivares generation come to the the wake: a former dean, a former guerrilla fighter, a former police chief. And el *Pato* Vértíz, who's barely a shell of his former self. First Olivares was el *Pato's* disciple, then his secretary, and finally his protector as age yellowed el *Pato's* teeth, flattened his nose, and added an unseemly bulge to his midsection.

I see el *Pato* at the rear of the funeral parlor when I arrive. He sees me too. At the risk of being ignored he chances a wave across the roomful of bald and graying heads. He knows I can't ignore the history we share. That history hurts.

I'm drunk out of my mind on a sofa in the house of Liliana Montoya, who is also drunk. I'm twenty-four and she's twenty-two. Lilliana tells me her younger sister's been dishonored and she, Liliana, had the creep who did it killed. She arranged it through the dirty old man who's been her lover for several months, a doctor of criminology named Roberto Gómez Vértiz, better known as el *Pato*, the man waving at me from across the room.

Liliana tells me about her crime at the end of a family party that lasts until dawn. She's still living in her mother's house, having not yet moved in with el *Pato*. She's so drunk that she has to throw up and must rush to the bathroom. Then she falls asleep in my lap. Although I attribute her dire scheme to alcohol, I record it in a notebook the next day. Years go by without my knowing if what Liliana told me on the couch is true or not, if it's a product of my inebriation or hers. I'm inclined to believe it's true; it's a plot Liliana could hatch. I've always known it's a scene with the seeds of a novel in it.

I must now disclose that I'm a writer. I don't mince words, and I stay on point. I cleave to my biases, and I don't digress. Reading what I write isn't enough, you must also doubt.

El *Pato* Vértiz heads the clique of faculty members who do the government's bidding at the university post-1968, toadies the rest of the university despises.

He's called el *Pato* Vértiz because he waddles like a duck, but that's the only way he resembles a duck. Otherwise he's like a cat or a crocodile. At forty, when he beds Liliana, his dry skin and thinning hair bespeak the man he'll be at sixty. He has dark skin, darker lips, and buck teeth that really could be an incipient duckbill. He smokes vanilla-scented cigarettes with black wrappings and gold filters and lords over the law school like an invisible god. He teaches criminology, but what he really does is run the place. He's the gray eminence of student brawls, the protector of gangs, and the alchemist who makes sure student groups elect the right leaders. He knows everything there is to know about promising undergraduates, including a bit of dirt on them or their parents. He intuits the unscrupulous adult in the dissolute youth and spots flickers of ambition and venality in recently registered coeds according to the length of their skirts. He could have been an omniscient novelist, but he's too corrupt. At heart he's only a flatterer and a cop. He's onto Liliana Montoya the minute he sees her. She has long legs and eyes that sparkle.

Liliana is the younger sister of my friend Rubén Montoya. Their widowed mother had fourteen children: six boys and eight girls. The mother is missing two front teeth, and when she eats she purses her lips over the gap where they used to be. I borrowed her dark eyes, and, as best I could, her heart for a story about a mother looking for her son in a police lockup. When she learns he's been killed, she adopts a prisoner who happens to be nearby and makes him her substitute son.

The day Rubén's mother meets me she dubs me Ricardo after her deceased son, Liliana's twin. Ricardo dies when a busload of pilgrims going to the Shrine of the Virgin of Chalma rolls over. It isn't the bus Ricardo's supposed be on for Mexico City; he isn't a pilgrim. At the bus station in Morelia he boards the bus to Chalma on a whim. He just wants to see the shrine and meet the pilgrims. He meets death.

I become a friend of Liliana's family thanks to her brother Rubén, who's my classmate at the university. The day I walk through the door of the Montoya house with its high ceilings and old rooms near the Buenavista train station, Liliana's mother says: "You're just like my Ricardo." She makes the sign of the cross over my forehead, mouth and chest, then gazes into my eyes as if looking for a secret only she can see. While Rubén's mother gives me her triple blessing my eye is on a shaft of light at the far side of the dining room. It's early spring in the city, and the sun shines down on the spot where a barefoot girl is standing. The radiance makes the thin fabric of her dress translucent, creating a silhouette of her body. It traces the high arches of her feet, her long legs and full hips; she has a child's narrow waist and long arms as well rounded as her legs. Her girlishly bright eyes sparkle. She's amused at the sight of her mother kissing me. She has white teeth and the high cheekbones of a cat. Under the bright light her black hair seems almost blue. She looks on as her mother kisses me. She already knows all about me. Everything.

As proof of my adoption Mrs. Montoya gives me a key to the front door. Lilliana and I reward her trust with incest. One afternoon I arrive at the house with its huge kitchen and long hallways to find Liliana washing her underwear in the sink. It's Thursday of Holy Week. Her mother has gone to Morelia with the rest of the family. Lilliana has decided not to go and is alone in the house. She says, "I'm out of fresh underwear, take a look."

She lifts her skirt so I can see. Her thighs and stomach are brown, her pubic hair jet black, almost blue. I'll never forget that body, that hair. Nor will they forget me. Keep this in mind from now on, this is not a moment I'll forget. Liliana sits on the sink and opens herself to me. She's the goddess of moisture. She smells of freshly cut firewood, of the detergent she uses to wash her underwear, and the perfumed sweetness of a strip joint. She giggles like a parrot while I'm in her. She says she's going to tell on me, tell her mom what I do to her, what I'm leaving inside her by the liter. The words she speaks that afternoon become a code: "I'm telling my mom on you." From then on she'll repeat these words as an invitation. If she speaks them when we're alone it means I can lift her skirt and enter right away because she's all ready. If she says them in front of her siblings or mother after dinner, or when saying goodnight, it means I should pretend I'm going to the bathroom where she'll be sitting on the sink or leaning against the wall with her skirt up.

El *Pato*'s wave brings everything back to me. I don't approach him to say hello. I do my best to pretend I can't work my way to the back of the room because I'm sidetracked into conversations with others. But el *Pato* is sly, he slithers through the crowd, and I hear his voice cascading down my back.

"How are you, old friend?"

When I turn around his large trembling hand is extended.

"How are you?" he repeats.

I say fine..., and how's he?

"I live and learn, my friend. Who would have guessed that you'd turn out to be our writer?"

He wheezes when he talks due to asthma or emphysema. One eyelid droops more than the other. The half-open eye has a deadly stare. His lashes are long and curled, the one sign of life on his face.

"We must talk," he says. "You've forgotten us."

I have no idea what he means by "us" because I never see him or anyone close to him. I think he uses the plural to set the stage for what he'll later describe as a "reencounter."

Making his way through the mourners, *Felo* Fernández comes to my rescue. "Our friend the Rector wants to say hello to you," he says.

El *Pato* Vértiz is standing next to me, he hastens to clarify: "Former dean."

The barb is deft and quick. *Felo* parries it with his inimitable humor. "We're all grateful for the way the 'former dean' did his job. He taught us how to fatten our bank accounts."

El *Pato's* guffaw shatters the prevailing murmur in the room. His laugh belies his years as if old age were just a disguise for his cheerful and predatory soul.

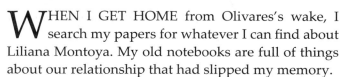

WHEN I GET HOME from Olivares's wake, I search my papers for whatever I can find about Liliana Montoya. My old notebooks are full of things about our relationship that had slipped my memory.

My incestuous dalliances with Liliana Montoya begin, as already noted, one Thursday in April 1972 on the kitchen sink in her house. Shortly before that scene, in February, Liliana turned 18. I turned 20 that January. Two years later, in 1974, Liliana enrolls in the school of political science, and I'm in my third year of philosophy and letters. Come 1976 Liliana's in her second year of political science, and she's going around with el *Pato* Vértiz. El *Pato's* twenty years her senior, and he takes her to a candlelight dinner with violins at a restaurant best known for its snob appeal. Before then she'd only dated me and others her own age. Her promiscuity bothers me, but my jealousy is no match for my libido. She's always saying she wants to leave home and move in with me, but I have no money and no place to put her. Besides, I want to write, and Liliana doesn't strike me as the sort of wife a writer ought to have. Her speaking voice is strident, her singing voice is unforgettable, but her laugh is loud and vulgar, and she laughs at anything, especially me. In public, in the metro, wherever. Her cackle makes people look away, but they can't help watching her out of the corners of their eyes, she's so pretty, but what a horrible laugh.

I now turn to Liliana's younger sister. Her name's Dorotea. My earliest memory of her is as a girl in a violet school uniform and sagging bobby socks. From the body of a young girl the shape of a woman is beginning to blossom but has yet to bloom. She's tall and slender. She has the smooth, nut-brown skin that painters such as Romero de Torres try to replicate in their dusky female subjects. Although she seems bright and alert, Dorotea's expression doesn't quite hide an underlying sense of boredom. Her smile is ironic as if she's bracing herself for the scorn of others. It's hard to imagine this girl in the clutches of someone who would abuse her.

One night she comes to Liliana with the veins in her wrist partially slit and says she's been dishonored. Dorotea is 18, the age Liliana was at the time of our first coupling. Dorotea's boyfriend is twenty years older than she is, an age gap identical to the one between el *Pato* Vértiz and Liliana when he began taking her out. Liliana listens closely as Dorotea tells how her boyfriend humiliates her. The sisters call him el *Catracho*, a slur often applied to Hondurans. Dorotea's ashamed of the things el *Catracho* makes her do. He forces her to take pills and inhale substances that weaken her will. He makes her dress up as an old woman or a little girl, a nun or the Virgin. Dorotea is in tears as she describes how she's been mistreated. Worse yet, Liliana thinks, he's not even Mexican. She can't say why, but his being a foreigner makes him doubly evil in her eyes. The next day she tells el *Pato* Vértiz to get rid of el *Catracho*. El *Pato* laughs and tells her she's crazy. He offers to have el *Catracho* beaten up and deported. Liliana looks at el *Pato* as if he's misunderstood her. She repeats herself. At first el *Pato* can't believe she's serious, her words frighten him. He doesn't know what to say. Days go by, and Liliana doesn't let up. When is el *Catracho* going to be killed? El *Pato's* non-committal. Liliana goes on strike, she refuses to sleep with el *Pato* as long as el *Catracho* is alive. It takes a month and a half for el *Pato* to learn his lesson. There's nothing he can do about Liliana's abstinence. He's as fatally drawn to Liliana as I am though in a more unusual way. El *Pato* thinks he's master of his own fate; I think I am what I am with no delusions about being anything more.

One day el *Pato* demands that Liliana come back. The next day he pleads with her. There comes a night when he admits to himself that he's desperate for her. He's as addicted to Liliana as I am. One evening, while she's having supper with her family in the San Rafael district, he phones to say, "Mission accomplished."

Later he shows her photos of a man with a bullet hole in his head. One eye is half-open, and he's lying in a pool of blood. Upon seeing the photos, Dorotea bursts into tears. It's el *Catracho*.

As I said, I heard about this from Liliana after a roaring drunk from which I woke up hungover and scared. Scared by what I'd heard and frightened by the woman I heard it from, I make up my mind to stay away from Liliana, to stop seeing her. I don't realize such things are not for me to decide.

I don't go near her during the Christmas holiday that year, and I don't return her calls. I'm already out of college, and there's no need for me to cross paths with her. But Liliana shows up at my January 14 birthday party anyway. As usual, the celebration culminates in a round of serious barhopping. I wake up in a fleabag hotel with Liliana beside me. I have no memory of the previous day, but I do recall the day before that. I particularly remember the sinister detail Liliana adds when she tells me about the murder of el *Catracho* for a second time. She and Dorotea go to see the body she says, and Dorotea prods it with her foot to make sure he's dead.

Once again I'm horrified, and I hasten to get away from Liliana. She comes looking for me, but I refuse to be found. Finally, I write her a letter asking her for a truce. Couldn't we stop seeing each other for a few months? I need to clear my head, I'm going on a trip, I ought to write a book. Liliana writes back, "This isn't a war, asshole."

But it is, it's begun to be.

The day Liliana calls to say she's going on vacation with el *Pato* Vértiz for the first time, she adds, "If you ask, I'll go with you."

I don't have enough money, and I don't want to take her anywhere. Thinking about where she can take me makes me dizzy. That's where I want to go. When it comes to Liliana, it's the story of my life.

When she finishes college, el *Pato's* graduation gift is an apartment. Liliana doesn't turn it down. Before moving, she sends me a note telling me what she's up to. At the end she writes, "If you ask, I'll move in with you."

I don't ask, but I call her to say don't move in with el *Pato*.

"What'll you give me?" she replies. I tell her I can't give her anything, but she shouldn't move in with el *Pato*.

"The train comes by just once in a lifetime,

Serranito."

My last name is Serrano, and this is the first time she calls me Serranito. Her use of the diminutive says it all. I'm afraid of the woman I love, and that makes me less of a man in her eyes. And in mine too.

The following year, while distancing myself from Liliana, I marry Aurelia Aburto, a colleague at the newspaper I've begun working for. It's a left-wing paper from which I'm fired and where I make enemies for life. Starting with Aurelia.

On a Friday in September 1980, as I write in my notebook, I see Liliana in her role as the partner of el *Pato* Vértiz for the first time. It happens in the all-night eatery on Tlacoquemécatl Street not far from my house in the Mexico City district of Valle de Ciudad México. The eatery on Tlacoquemécatl serves spicy soups and barbecued ribs, and I'm in the habit of going there for an early breakfast. I normally order scrambled eggs with pork sausage, tortillas warmed on the griddle, and coffee brewed with cinnamon in a clay pot. I have breakfast early before settling into a morning of writing. I write from 8 a.m. to 3 p.m. when my shift begins at the paper. It's dawn when Liliana and el *Pato* come to the eatery after a night out drinking. I see her laughing and singing at el *Pato's* side. She throws herself into his arms, rubs his neck, kisses his throat, gives him a drink from the flask of rum she takes from his pocket. Neither Liliana nor el *Pato* see me because I slip into the kitchen the minute they arrive. From a hiding place redolent of fried food and steaming soup, I watch Liliana and el *Pato* in the complicit company of a cook named Chole.

At the end of that year I break up with Aurelia

Aburto and raise the curtain on my days as a lone wolf. Now I arrive at the eatery on Tlacoquemécatl with the partner I've spent the night drinking and dancing with. I make it a point to stay away from Liliana, but I do hear about her. Tales of promiscuity, alcohol and money under the aegis of el *Pato*. *Felo* Fernández keeps me informed.

In my opinion, el *Pato* has corrupted Liliana just as el *Catracho* corrupted her sister Dorotea. But no one has put out a contract on el *Pato* the way Liliana did on el *Catracho*. Liliana has looked out for Dorotea better than I looked out for Liliana.

One day *Felo* Fernández tells me el *Pato* has twice done time in sanatoriums where they dry out alcoholics. I'm happy to hear it. A year later I learn, thanks to an ad in the back pages of a newspaper, that Liliana's the featured singer in a bar. I make a clandestine visit in time for the last show of the night. From a dark table at the back of the bar I watch her light up the stage. Her silver lip gloss shimmers like varnish under the lone spotlight. Her white gown is cut just low enough to display the tops of her small round breasts. My eyes fill with tears as she sings. I cry, pay, and leave before the end of her song.

About this time the newspaper fires me, and I marry my second wife, a woman I'll call Josefa. I publish a novel based on my time at the paper, and my ex-colleagues are mortally offended by how I portray them. They call me a failed journalist, a traitor to a profession I have no right to slander. The book is reasonably successful. The publishing house where I work after the newspaper — where Josefa also works — offers me a job at their home office in Barcelona where

I spend six years. Josefa buys an apartment and has a miscarriage. I write and publish two novels.

Felo Fernández writes often, and through him I gather the little I know about Liliana in those years, her promiscuity, her drinking, her liaisons. She opens a bar with one well-heeled boyfriend then a gift shop with another. El *Pato's* left in the lurch. He loses Liliana and goes back to his first wife. Politically and professionally, he's dependent on Olivares. He's a shadow of his former self.

So, in my own way, am I.

Josefa leaves me when our attempt at reconciliation goes awry during a vacation in Melilla. I return from Spain after the divorce. I'm thirty-six at the time. Liliana's thirty-four, el *Pato* Vértiz is fifty-four.

I run into Liliana one afternoon at a restaurant that no longer exists on the southern edge of Mexico City: an eccentric place called *Los comerciales.*

The waiters put clown hats on patrons' heads, serenade them with verses of "Happy Birthday," serve them cakes with lighted candles, and smother them in congratulations. You eat well at *Los comerciales* too. At her table Liliana's carrying on a lively conversation with a man with dyed black hair. He's wearing a blazer with a turquoise handkerchief that matches his tie. Liliana makes a beeline across the room to greet me. She pokes at my chest and arms with both her hands as if daring me to fight.

"You're so skinny," she says. "How come you're so skinny?"

Her breath is laced with the sweet scent of her burnt orange lipstick and a whiff of the tequila she's drinking, or drank last night.

"We need to get together, creep."

She gives me her phone number and writes mine down. At her table, she deliberately sits where I can look at her without her having to look at me. That's what she wants, that's what I do. The cut of her green sheath leaves her arms bare while accentuating her trim waist and slender hips. She knows I'm looking at her. She's well aware of her long legs and the effect they have when she walks. She runs her left hand through her hair, brushing it over her shoulders and lifting it up to show off her neck, then she lets it fall down her back with the insouciance of a diva.

AT THE TIME I'M WORKING on a book about the Huitzilac Massacre. I have a Guggenheim grant to write about the Huitzilac Massacre. It happened on October 3, 1927. Soldiers and civilians accused of plotting against the government were shot. They were killed in cold blood with no trial. Out of respect for a superstition honored by journalists and writers alike I decide to visit the place I'll be writing about. I prepare for my pilgrimage with long hours poring over books and chronicles. I do what I can to make the trip to Huitzilac worthwhile. It's neither a difficult or complicated task since Huitzilac is just a few kilometers from Mexico City. The hard part will be finding anything of use at a massacre site now buried beneath a blanket of urban sprawl. Nothing marks the place where, one after the other, the condemned were forced to kneel and then executed. But I'm making the ritual site visit anyway.

The night before the trip Liliana phones me. She says, "I know you wouldn't call me because you always run away from me, which is why I'm calling you."

I ask how she knows I wouldn't call her.

"Because you looked like a priest sneaking out of the restaurant."

I ask what made me look like a priest at the restaurant.

"You were horny and scared, Serranito. Like a

priest with a hard on. When am I going to see you?"

I ask if she'd like to go to Huitzilac in the morning.

"Huitzilac?" she snickers. "What will we do in Huitzilac, creep? There's nothing to do in Huitzilac."

I tell her I'm researching a massacre, which draws another snicker. "That's all?"

This time she laughs out loud, and as always her laugh makes me cringe. She stops laughing and agrees to go. "All right. If it has to be Huitzilac, then Huitzilac it is. What time are you coming for me?"

I tell her eight in the morning.

"Fine."

I ask for her address.

"Everything's changed but my address."

At eight on the dot I pick her up at the building where el *Pato* Vértiz bought her an apartment, where she's lived for years without el *Pato*. She looks as if she hasn't slept as she gets in the car; she smells of alcohol and chatters like a parrot. Her eyes are red and alluringly puffy. I neither remember nor wrote down what she said.

There are lots of motels on the toll-free road through Cuernavaca to Huitzilac. When we pass the second one Liliana says, "Is this where we investigate the Huitzilac massacre, Serranito?" I turn into the next motel we come to. "There's one room here I won't go into," she says and points at it with her finger. "Any other will do."

I pass the forbidden room and pull into the garage under a different one. Above each garage is a room with a double bed, a jacuzzi, a television, and purple curtains and carpets.

In the room Liliana cautions me not to order

drinks, "Because they water them down here. We need to order sealed bottles."

She phones for champagne without specifying the brand. Without waiting for it to arrive, she starts the jacuzzi. "I'll take a bath and get ready for you," she says.

It's nine in the morning. She takes a bath that lasts until the champagne comes. I've ordered breakfast for two: juice, scrambled eggs, toast, and a pot of coffee. Liliana emerges from the jacuzzi wrapped in purple motel towels. Though ready for me, she breaks open the champagne to drink with breakfast. We eat the eggs and drink the champagne. It's my first drink in many years. We do nothing except eat, drink and talk. I'm grateful for that. All I want this morning is to talk to her, to ask how she remembers me and what I meant to her. My recollections of myself are problematical. I need other people's memories of me because I'm a writer who can't look himself in the eye. Lilliana's self-confidence is like a mirror. What she says to me that morning in the motel is, "If you had any balls, creep, I might have been your wife. If you had balls I'd have worshipped you like the nonexistent God the whole world is looking for."

She capitalizes God with her voice, she has a way of capitalizing words in general.

We leave the motel full of breakfast and champagne. We go on to Huitzilac as my project demands. I listen, look, and take notes of things I can use, including the way Liliana sums up the gratuitousness of the massacre:

"Those people got screwed coming and going."

Night has fallen by the time we get back to the

city, and Liliana makes the move that makes the day. She invites me in for a drink. We return to where I picked her up in the morning, a ten-story building that stands alone in a valley of squat houses next to the Río de la Piedad Viaduct. It's a building that can be seen from a distance and, from inside it, you see far into the distance because, instead of walls, its four sides are glass from the ground up. Liliana's apartment—the one el *Pato* Vértiz bought for her—is on the sixth floor. Now that el *Pato* Vértiz is gone, she shows me around. In the bedroom there's a round bed with a silver eiderdown. "Here we get it on," Liliana says.

The sala has a professional-looking bar with a mirror and a display of shelved bottles. She serves herself a vodka on the rocks and downs it in a single gulp. "All right," she says, "what are you drinking?" I answer the usual. Cuba Libre, she recalls. She asks what I've been doing, what am I doing now? I start to tell her while she starts taking her clothes off. She continues to strip as she walks towards the picture window in the sala of her apartment. The lights of the city shimmer through the glass. At this time of night, with the lights on, her apartment glows like an illuminated cube. Liliana's body must be seen to be appreciated. Anyone looking up from below would see a long back, a slender waist, sturdy legs, and well turned arms. Looking at her from the front, I see two small breasts, a flat stomach, and a thatch of black, almost blue pubic hair.

She's still a beautiful woman, maybe even more beautiful now than the girl with brown skin and Asian features she once was. Standing before me with open arms, she's at ease with the pleasure and pain that go with her looks:

"Just like before, Serranito. Like it used to be."

I'm not aroused. Ten o'clock comes and goes in the round bed. She hasn't stopped pouring vodka for herself and Cuba Libres for me. We hardly ate in Huitzilac, and we're both hungry.

"How about a steak at Pepe's, Serranito? You remember Pepe's?"

I remember Pepe's, a long-gone steakhouse on the traffic circle at the intersection of Insurgentes and Mixcoac. A young waiter named Alfonso greets me with a familiarity that intrigues Liliana.

"Who did you cuddle up with here, Serranito?"

She's caught the scent of Aurelia Aburto, who used to accompany me to this restaurant at least once a week after work at the newspaper. I broke up with Aurelia Aburto long ago, but time doesn't matter to Liliana's surprisingly acute sense of smell.

We drink a bottle of wine with our steak. It's midnight by the time we leave. A fresh breeze blows Liliana's hair over her forehead. "Take me dancing," she says. "You remember the Buca Bar?"

I remember the all-night dive on Bucareli that shut down years ago. Once, through the blare of trumpets and song, *Felo* Fernández showed off his talent for chewing glass while improvising monologues on Mexican history. According to the monologue: when soldiers ruled, wars were lost; when lawyers ruled, laws were broken; and when economists ruled, the country went broke.

Liliana orders a bottle of rum, seal intact, and breaks its plastic foil with her fingernail. By three in the morning the bottle is half empty, and we've sweated off some of the alcohol attempting to dance to the random strains of "In-A-Gadda-Da-Vida" and "Caballo Viejo." Bucareli Street is deserted when we leave Buca Bar. Trash blows in the wind. The tracks of trolleys that no longer run glimmer under the pale light of the street lamps.

"Take me to Cingaros," Liliana says.

Before it closed Cingaros was an illegal bar where whores and drunks from the Zona Rosa used to greet the dawn. A waitress named Minerva welcomes Liliana with squeals of joy. In her joy I catch the scent of tips left by el *Pato* Vértiz and his successors. There's no music here, only the din of drunken voices scraping over each other in fits of anger, boasting, mirth or stupidity. A man at the table next to ours accuses a woman of disrespecting him. "Ma-marry me. Or-or are you ju-just t-trying to make me look fu-foolish?"

Minerva brings an ice bucket and Coca Colas to go with the half bottle of rum from Buca Bar that Liliana sets on the table. Minerva returns a few moments later with a cigarette tray that hangs suspended between her stomach and the strap around her neck. She's short and skinny with a mane of black hair as thick as a lion's. She opens a compartment in her cigarette tray to reveal sub-compartments full of pills. Liliana takes two in the palm of her hand and pops them into her mouth before pouring us two Cubas, pale drinks that sting our lips because they're more rum than Coke.

"Since you're into killing, Serranito, let me tell you about the bastard I had killed," Liliana says.

For the third time she tells me how she had a man killed for dishonoring her sister Dorotea. I'd listened closely the first two times, and I listened closely now.

In those days I could transcribe what I heard verbatim, a skill I've since lost. I willingly listen to her tale in Cingaros, a spot now gone from the city and from memory.

Liliana forgets she's told me the story twice before. She tells it from beginning to end as if for the first time, and in the retelling she adds a sinister detail. She says she witnesses the execution of el *Catracho*. What's more, she tells his murderers exactly how she wants him killed. Dorotea doesn't remember a thing about this, she says. Dorotea's happily married, she has two lovers and a son who seemed retarded until he turned out to be a mathematical genius.

The story erases the alcoholic fog from my head. We're going to find something to eat, I tell her.

"I know just the place," she says.

So do I. We end the night in the somewhat seedy cafe at the Tlacoquemécatl Inn, the place from whose kitchen I once spied on Liliana and el *Pato*. We walk the few blocks from the cafe to my apartment and sleep until noon. By the time I wake up, Liliana has bathed, fried sausages, and gone through my liquor cabinet where the only alcohol she finds is an ancient bottle of rum without a cap. She hands me a Cuba with rum from the bottle with the missing cap and plies me with sausages. She has me change my clothes and take her to her apartment so she too can change.

From Liliana's we go to the bar at the Jena, a bygone hotel on Morelos Street. After the Jena we eat at Ambassadeurs, a bygone restaurant on Paseo de la Reforma next to the newspaper *Excelsior*. From Ambassadeurs we go to the El Patio Cabaret, the site of José José's penultimate performances. From El

Patio we go to El Bar del León in the historic district, a ghost of times past where a waiter named Luis, whom everybody, including Liliana, calls *Monsieur*, brings us a sealed bottle of rum and a bucket of iced Coca Colas to drink while listening to a combo of antiquated musicians. With dawn approaching, we head for the crowded ballroom on La Palma where morning never comes and you can dance and drink until noon. Under a bleary sun we stumble out of the night and into the bustling city like drunken ghosts. We stagger into a nearby hotel to sleep. When I wake up in late afternoon Liliana is straddling me, freshly bathed and shampooed. The light is facing us as we leave the hotel. Our clothes are a mess, but we're ready and willing to take on the world outside.

I don't remember much about the next two days. Just a scribbled list of the places we went in a notebook. From the hotel on Palma we go to Puerta del Sol, a bar that used to be on the same street. From Puerto del Sol we go to the Prendes Restaurant on Sixteenth of September. From the Prendes we go to Salón Riviére where the dancing starts early. From Salón Riviére we go to Vértiz Street, home of the Artists' Club whose explicit sex shows are now found only in the lost pages of obscure cultural journals. From there we go to the Catalonia, a hotel in the Doctores district where the rooms rent by the hour. I come to in a bed in the district's General Hospital with tubes in one arm and an inner peace that feels like death.

Liliana is nowhere to be found.

ISPEND THE NEXT TWO YEARS at the University of Iowa writing my book about Huitzilac. I go the whole time without hearing or wanting to hear anything about Liliana. I finish the book. The day of its release in Mexico City she gets in line to have her copy signed at the end of the book party. Her black eyes smolder with her unique mix of pride and diffidence. Or—just as possibly—with a snort of cocaine. Her Prince Valiant haircut and the tailoring of her sand-colored suede suit make her look like a mischievous child. The plum-colored scarf at her throat matches her lipstick.

When she gets to the head of the line she says, "My name's not in the book, but I know I'm in there."

I dedicate her copy, "To Liliana, who's in the book though her name's not there."

She reads the dedication and says, "Shall I wait for you so we can talk about old times?"

I look for her when I finish signing, but she's left. I still have the phone number of her old apartment where we met three years ago. No one answers when I call that night or in the following days. When I go to look for her in her apartment, the doorman tells me she hasn't lived there for months. A bout of nostalgia drives me to look for her in the Montoyas' old house in the San Rafael district. It's now a kindergarten.

I look up *Felo* Fernández. He doesn't know where to find Liliana, but he does know where el *Pato* is.

He's holed up in a minor government office run by Olivares, whose death is yet to come.

I'm in physical need of Liliana Montoya.

I blink, and the years fast-forward to a call from *Felo* Fernández.

"Boss, it's been four years since we talked. Pardon the delay. I'm calling because yesterday our old pal Olivares kicked the bucket. The wake's at Gayosso's on Félix Cuevas. Maybe we'll run into each other."

Olivares's death surprises me less than four years of not hearing from *Felo* and doing without Liliana.

"It seems like yesterday," I tell *Felo* Fernández.

Life goes by in a heartbeat, and so do we.

As I said, the presence of el *Pato* Vértiz at Olivares's wake reinvigorates my quest for Liliana Montoya. I lost track of her in the four years since my book about Huitzilac came out. If there's a whiff of Liliana anywhere, I tell myself, I'll find it among the friends of Olivares and el *Pato*, who, I suppose, longs for her as much as I do. *Felo* Fernández is the first step on my search for her, and I have him update me on el *Pato* and the now-departed Olivares.

Felo gets back to me nearly empty-handed. "The last anyone heard of Liliana Montoya she ran a hotel in Antigua, Guatemala. Then she had a bar in Los Cabos where she sang. That's it."

I ask if el *Pato's* the source of what he tells me.

"El *Pato* tries to keeps tabs on her, but he's lost sight of her. No one else is looking for her except you. I share your sexual and literary weakness for her, but I'd advise you to keep your distance. She's a nefarious woman, a temptress who left a whole generation in her wake. When did you say you saw her last?"

I tell him again, "It's been four years."

"For your peace of mind and the good of the nation, get over her. Everyone who tries to screw her loses half his prick."

Felo's right. Liliana has washed in and out of my life on waves of disaster. She bides her time in the back of my mind. I've loved this woman more than I've feared her, but fear has always won.

Her story about the killing of el *Catracho* gives me bad dreams for years. Sometimes I'm his designated murderer; sometimes I've already killed him and am running from the law like a hunted animal. I wake up one morning in the grip of a horrifying revelation: I'm the one who killed el *Catracho*. I did it because Liliana told me to, then put what I did out of my schizophrenic mind. I'm sweating and trembling. It takes me several seconds to come to myself and admit that my nightmare has grown more vivid and maddening over the years. I remember deciding to investigate the death of el *Catracho*. It's a commitment I also remember forgetting.

After Olivares's wake I again decide to investigate the death of el *Catracho*. Readdressing this enigma is one way to pick up Liliana's trail. It's an indirect way to be sure, and I might actually prefer not to find her, but maybe I'll run across her in the course of the search.

I begin by recapitulating what I already know.

Liliana told me about el *Catracho's* murder three times. Each time she says she's the one who asks el *Pato* Vértiz to kill him. That never varies. In the first version, el *Pato* has him killed and takes photos of the body to prove it. In the second version, Liliana and her sister Dorotea go to see the corpse, and Dorotea pokes it with her foot to make sure he's dead. In the third version, Liliana is present at the execution and specifies how el *Catracho* is to be killed.

I write and destroy a short novel based on the second and third versions. I don't publish it because I'm afraid of el *Pato* Vértiz. He's an animal Liliana may have trained, but he's no lap dog. In the novel I say the Liliana figure is as distraught as her wronged sister. The narrator takes it for granted that such transgressions are beyond redemption and that the two sisters will always be harnessed with guilt. But, in the third version, Liliana unintentionally stresses that the transgression has no consequences. She feels no remorse, and neither does Dorotea, who has a husband to provide for her, two lovers who dote on her, and a near genius of a son.

For her part, Liliana has dumped el *Pato* and had affairs with other equally profitable lovers. It could be said that misfortune armored her against suffering and made her immune to blame. For Liliana Montoya and her sister Dorotea, what matter are results; guilt is irrelevant.

The notes I've kept from my penultimate encounter with Liliana—our trip to Huitzilac—include the date of el *Catracho*'s murder: February 14, 1978, Valentine's Day. "We gave him a Valentine's gift of love," Liliana says in my notes.

I spend a whole day in the periodicals library going over the crime pages of newspapers from that date. I find nothing. I turn from newspapers to magazines. The daily bloodletting is staggering: crimes, accidents, catastrophes, record-setting mass killings. I'm horrified and numb by the end of the morning. A headline says "a foreign journalist" whom I met has gone missing on the beaches of Oaxaca. A few pages later another headline discloses the death of a foreign tourist in a sleazy bar. Later I come across headlines about the death of "a models' agent," also a foreigner, who drowned in Manzanillo. People from other countries seem to gain a measure of notoriety in these pages. I keep an eye out for the word "foreigner" in the magazine I happen to be paging through. In a flicker of chauvinism, I wonder if this toxic brew of foreign blood and fatal accidents might make an odd kind of sense. I go back to the volume for 1978 and read only the stories about dead foreigners. I find nothing. I ask for 1979. In a headline from the first week of March I read: "Foreigner shot dead in revenge killing." The following story says:

> Honduran lowlife Cataldo Peña found dead; lured two young prostitutes to his den.

The story goes on:

> Fellow lowlifes appear to have dispatched him from their shameful profession with two bullets to the chest and one to the head. His days of trafficking unsuspecting young innocents to customers as twisted as he are over. The unsavory doings of this despicable Honduran were a stain on the good name of a beautiful neighboring country.

Adding:

> Investigations are ongoing in the offices of the Anti-Crime Division (formerly the Secret Service).

The Honduran is a big fish, and the authorities are working to uncover possible links between him and other criminal groups.

I correct the year of my search and revisit the dailies. I begin at March 1979 and draw a blank. I go back to February and find nothing on the 15th or 16th, but on Saturday the 17th I find a story about the death of "a pimp named Clotaldo Peña." City police are looking into possible links between this crime and a band of Colombian thugs long active in the city. I check the dailies one by one through July 1979 to no avail. I return to the magazine and check the whole year. Not a line.

I pay *Felo* Fernández and ask if he knows anyone who could get me access to the 1979 files of the renowned DIPD, the Criminal Investigation and Prevention Division that was disbanded in 1983.

Felo Fernández takes me to his old classmate Ricardo Antúnez, a longtime protégé of el *Pato* Vértiz who later became el *Pato's* mortal enemy. As the city's first civilian security chief, Antúnez was an absolute disaster. Ten years ago, during his glory days, I had a minor but unforgettable run-in with him. While dining at the fashionable Cicero Restaurant, I publicly refused a bottle of wine he sent from his table to mine. Antúnez tells *Felo* he'd be glad to see me provided our meeting takes place at the Cicero Restaurant.

He and *Felo* are waiting for me when I arrive. He greets me with open arms. He says this will be a friendly meal, but, to make sure it is, I should lay my cards on the table right now. He asks me what I want. I repeat what I told *Felo* Fernández. I want a copy of the case file of a Honduran named Clotaldo or Cataldo Peña, who was murdered in mid-February 1979.

Antúnez has a walrus mustache and a scalp as smooth as a billiard ball. He has long curled eyelashes and thick hairy fingers. Though he looks affable, his demeanor is icy. He has a huge watch on his thick hairy wrist. He doesn't ask why I'm interested in the case, but he leaves no doubt he's familiar with it.

"I'll get you the file, count on it. But what do you want to know, what happened or what's in the case file?"

I tell him both. Antúnez hastens to explain his question.

"What's in the file isn't necessarily what happened. The court record is one thing, the police blotter is another. The police blotter is more accurate."

I'm slow to grasp that Antúnez is making me an offer. *Felo* Fernández sees I'm lost and explains. "What Antúnez is asking is if you want him to look up a comandante from those days, someone with first-hand knowledge of the case."

I say, yes, naturally.

"That'll cost you a bottle of wine," Antúnez says with a yawn.

I agree. Antúnez scans the wine list and chooses a Spanish tinto, the most expensive wine on the menu. Olivares's old students never miss a trick. Antúnez keeps his word. A week later he sends me a photocopy of the file. Then he calls to invite me for another dinner and promises to pay for the wine. Once again we eat at Cicero's. While we're considering dessert we're approached by an elderly man who seems perfectly alert but whose clothes are wrinkled and threadbare. He has a mane of unkempt gray hair above a low forehead. As a waiter escorts him to our table, he looks the place over as if he were going to film it. He shakes hands with us before sitting down, his grip feels rough and calloused. We order dessert. Antúnez finishes his coffee and leaves when the conversation gets down to business.

"The two of you should talk alone."

Felo Fernández leaves with him. He has an affair of his own to take care of.

Being alone with the old comandante is like looking at a blank wall. The wall speaks, "Mr.Antúnez told me what you're looking for. Can we cut the bullshit and get to the point?"

THE CICERO IS A RESTAURANT where diners sometimes go for company as well as meals. There are tables where women linger after they eat to drink, smoke and talk. They laugh heartily at their own jokes. The laughs are intended as bait for men willing to pick up their tabs and invite them to their tables. The comandante looks over his right shoulder at one of these tables, then over his left shoulder. "Whores with hearts are so beautiful," he says. "They're our sirens, damn it."

His eyes seem to see straight through me. The corneas are pale around the edges. He seems to be watching me from a distance. His eyelids are veined and paper thin.

"Are you going to take notes?" he asks. I mustn't look too bright because he blinks at me in disgust and rephrases.

"Are you going to write down what I tell you? Will you be using my name?" I tell him no.

"You wouldn't know me if you saw me. Deal?" I'm not sure what he's trying to tell me, but I agree. "My name is Neri. I won't bullshit you. Agreed?"

I nod mechanically.

"What you already know about the case is true. Except two men died, not one. The guy you say is a foreigner is dead. But the other one is more important." I tell him there's no mention of a second fatality in the press or in the file.

"The important one is left out," he says. "I remember the case very well because I almost died that day. I went to a town in Morelos to look for a kidnapper. How he did it I don't know, but he turned the whole town against me. They were going to hang me in front of the church. The priest saved me. They almost lynched him, too. I got back to Mexico City at daybreak. In the squad room I was told to respond to a case in a whorehouse. It wasn't a whorehouse really, just a well furnished apartment in the San Rafael district. When I got there the owner—the man you're asking about—was already dead. The important one was being questioned, but the questioning got out of hand. Rather than try to explain why he was so banged up, the interrogators left him out of their report. 'A pimp was murdered here,' Comandante Reséndiz said. 'That's what happened, understood?' They got rid of the corpse and left me with the other dead guy, the one you're interested in. I was supposed to await further instructions. Morning came but no instructions. That was when the pressure began to build. It was a case that led to a lot of negotiation."

When I ask what he means by "negotiation," he describes a feud between the Secretary for Internal Security and the mayor of the city.

"The secretary was out to screw the mayor, and he thought we were the dirty-tricks squad. Which was right. In those years the prosecutor would ask the victims of major crimes if they wanted the culprits dead or alive. The answer was often dead, which is why we had a hit squad. Everyone in our unit belonged at one time or another. Some joined for the money, others to please their bosses."

I ask Neri if he was ever in the hit squad.

"Not for money. Only if the bad guys had it coming."

I ask how he knew they had it coming.

"When they were real creeps," he says. "Serial rapists or killers. We all have our standards. I can say for sure that I never killed anybody who didn't deserve it."

He asks for mineral water. He nods, shuts his eyes, then looks back at me.

"At the time the internal security secretary was trying to prove that the city prosecutor was ordering illegal executions. He wanted the mayor fired, and he was demanding an investigation of anything that resembled an execution. In the case you're asking about we said we were professional policemen acting in the line of duty when the important guy died."

I ask how this could be in the hit squad's line of duty. Comandante Neri explains further.

"Look, in those years groups of thugs not on the police watch list popped up every three or four months. If it was a gang no one knew about, it was an anomaly we had to take care of. In those days the police ruled the streets. We were the law, and the crooks were afraid of us. When law enforcement visited a thieves' market like Tepito, for example, small-time criminals swarmed about the comandante like flies: 'What's up, chief? How can we help you?' 'Well guys, there's been a burglary, and the lady of the house was raped. But the family's on our side, so the bastard who did it is going to get screwed. It's up to you guys to find out who it was.' And they would find out. Sometimes they'd even turn in the perpetrators themselves. The squad would hand them off to the authorities, and everybody was happy. In the case you speak of, the squad uncovered one of those gangs. They learned that the ringleader had been in the apartment where the dead guy—your dead guy—was. The cops went to the apartment, killed the owner, and waited for the ringleader to show up. When he did, they interrogated him. But, as I told you, the interrogation got out of hand."

I ask who the interrogators were.

"People from the old secret service. I was new at the time, kind of an apprentice. My job was to cover their asses, to clean up the place, and await further orders. Torturing the ringleader put them on the trail to the rest of the gang. That morning they recovered the stolen goods and killed them all. Then I was ordered to call the prosecutor's office and give them a story they could tell the press: the pimp was killed by his own clients, and we went looking for them because they were gang members. We didn't actually look for anybody, but there were no raised eyebrows and that was the end of it. I have clear memories of all this because, as I told you, I was nearly lynched the day before and also because what I'd seen scared me into quitting the police. Later on, after the housecleaning at DIPD, I went back to being a cop. The cleanup left the city without any cops. We had to rebuild the force from top to bottom. It was a total disaster. What we really did was dismantle the only real police force this country ever had. The comandantes owned the criminals. They ruled the underworld and were part of the underworld. It's the untold story nobody likes to bring up. But that's the way it was."

A woman's laugh echoes through the restaurant like the call of a mad bird. The comandante looks over his right shoulder to see where it came from. "That's quite a laugh," he says.

Neri's eyes are laughing at his own memory. I ask if he remembers everything that happened that night.

"I have a real good memory," he says. "On the job my memory could get me into trouble, but it could get me out of trouble too. I remember everything. Police work was all memory in those days. You never put a thing in writing."

I ask if anything unusual happened that night, if anyone had seen the cadaver.

"Yeah, a real sharp looking girl and the lawyer who was with her for muscle. I'd had a call from the prosecutor. He told me he'd sent them and to let them see the body. It seemed odd for such a young girl to be going around looking at corpses, but she came with my boss's friend, a university type."

I ask if the girl was alone, if there was one girl or two.

"Just one. Along with her muscle, the university guy. I used to know his name and who he worked for, but I've forgotten now. My memory of that night is crystal clear except for that."

I ask if he was with them while they looked at the body.

"No, I wasn't. I left them alone and stood guard outside the door. The guy rubbed me the wrong way. He tried to press a bill into my hand on his way out. I said, 'I'm not a waiter, sir.' I wouldn't take it. What got you so interested in this case?" I say the girl told me about it.

"Then you already knew what happened? Were you testing me?" I tell him I was testing the girl.

That makes him laugh. His wrinkled eyelids dim the sparkle in his eyes. His attention wanders back to the tables where the women are. He looks over one shoulder then the other.

"The logical way to leave a place like this would be with someone on your arm," he says. "What do you say we invite someone?"

He doesn't wait for my answer. He gets up and adjusts his belt. He's wearing cowboy boots and tight jeans. His legs look strong but bowed like two parentheses; he aches when he walks. His first words draw peals of laughter from the women at the table he approaches. They look to be around forty with blond hair and lots of mascara. Comandante Neri gestures and gauges how I react while continuing to say things that make the women laugh. One is wearing a green dress, the other is in yellow. They both have big breasts and low necklines.

Back in my apartment I wonder about Comandante Neri. His fatuity is matched only by his way with a story, and he clearly isn't swayed one way or the other by my interest in the case. As far as he's concerned, Liliana and el *Pato* Vértiz are not involved in the death of el *Catracho*. Their quest to avenge the stain on a family's honor is irrelevant to his tale of a police execution. But Neri's version does clarify certain things. First, Liliana didn't witness the killing of el *Catracho* and didn't determine the method of execution. Second, Dorotea didn't visit the scene of the crime, just Liliana.

What I overlook in my musings is the enormity

of what the comandante does confirm: el *Pato* had el *Catracho* killed on orders from Liliana and took her to see his body once he was dead. What Neri's version doesn't explain is the thing I care about the most: how did el *Pato* carry out Liliana's orders? The comandante has a different explanation for el *Catracho*'s death. The officers who kill him are actually looking for his whoring client, the leader of a gang that steals without their permission and must be taught a lesson. El *Catracho*'s a bystander they happen to kill, and I have no idea how to mesh the designs of the police with Liliana's whimsical homicide.

The prosecutor, who was Neri's boss and el *Pato*'s friend, could be a key to learning what really happened. But the prosecutor had died of old age and been buried with honor. I could go back to Neri, but neither el *Pato* nor Liliana figure in his recollection of the crime. Besides, I'd rather not have more to do with Comandante Neri.

Antúnez is another possibility, but I don't want to show him my hand and let him in on what I'm looking for. The fact is I'm not sure what I'm looking for, I only hope my search will lead me to Liliana. That's my real objective, the longing I hesitate to talk about. My lifelong attraction to her.

I'm left with no choice but to confront el *Pato* and squeeze the truth out of him. But I'm not up to doing that yet. My contempt for el *Pato* outweighs my curiosity.

LILIANA'S TRAIL GOES COLD in a Los Cabos hotel where someone heard her sing. Nobody knows what happened to her after that. Not *Felo* Fernández, not el *Pato* Vértiz, not the rest of the Olivares generation to whom she owes her legend and her ruin. Ruin is the place where I imagine she lives— or may no longer live—in the memory of a generation. Her disappearance is symptomatic, something I never stop thinking about. Failing to keep tabs on her is my fault. Blaming myself for losing track of her assuages my feelings of guilt.

The Olivares generation tells many tales about Liliana Montoya, and they tell them without affect or rancor. She lives on in their gossip. Their tales are subject to the ancient rule by which gossip, whether malicious or benign, confers notoriety. The adventures of Liliana circulate like old coins burnished by the touch of many hands. Gathering these coins turns the desk where I write into a gaming table. I don't say all the tales are true or that they harbor secret meanings. They simply evoke the things my obsessions gloss over, memories of a woman I can never have to myself and can never forget.

Among the Olivares generation the most popular stories are about the ways Liliana drives el *Pato* Vértiz mad. They marvel at how she does it while still just a girl. People who consider themselves his friends say the woman who could drive el *Pato* crazy must be something special. Being a friend of el *Pato's* isn't easy, but members of the Olivares generation all say they're his friends. To me the reason why is clear: el *Pato* has done each of them some undeserved favor, and he knows about all the skeletons in their closets.

The stories about el *Pato's* affair with Liliana make the rounds behind his back and include the following:

El *Pato's* wife has tried to kill herself by drinking a whole bottle of black ink. For her lethal libation she chooses Pelikan, the brand that fills more fountain pens than any other. She leaves a suicide note that does little to hide her motives. She spells Liliana's name in full with both her paternal (Montoya) and maternal (Giner) surnames. As a final flourish, she writes out the exact address of the apartment el *Pato* bought for Liliana in the building that towers above its low-slung neighbors along the Río Piedad Viaduct, one of the few in Mexico City with unobstructed views from all four sides. This, as his wife duly notes, is where el *Pato* sleeps several nights a week.

El *Pato* vows to break up with Liliana after the suicide attempt. He just can't go on seeing her after finding ink residue on the lips of his wife who begs him to come home. Drawing on her command of medieval literature, she insists he stop sleeping with that Maritornes, an archaic term for whore. Mrs. Vértiz has written several monographs on the life and times of Don Quijote and knows what she's talking about. El *Pato* announces to his friends and subordinates among the Olivares generation that he's granting his wife's wish, a major sacrifice given his great love for Liliana. A short time later he tells his friends and subordinates he'll be celebrating his birthday in the apartment he shares with Liliana.

Well before the party ends Liliana publicly tells el *Pato* he's free to go home to his wife and her shitty black lipstick. He needn't worry about Liliana because the party is throbbing with pricks for her to sleep with. She seats herself on the legs of Olivares, who isn't dead yet. He's still sober enough to know he's being used, and at the time is el *Pato's* private secretary. Olivares slides out from under Liliana, clambers to his feet, and pledges undying loyalty to his boss and friend. El *Pato* orders Liliana into the bedroom so he can talk to her alone, but she goes to the bar instead and pours herself a drink as if she hadn't heard him. According to the Olivares generation, el *Pato* tries to shrug off this act of defiance. Rather than go home, he spends the rest of his birthday chatting inanely with his guests as if all were well and nothing had changed. The only thing that didn't change is that when the party is over el *Pato* stays with Liliana until dawn.

Though el *Pato* moves out on his suicidal wife the following week, he does not move into the apartment he bought for Liliana. Now he only visits when invited. From the time el *Pato's* wife tries to kill herself until their affair comes to an end, Liliana is boss.

The Olivares generation weave el *Pato's* birthday party and his wife's botched suicide into a saga they never tire of reciting. Another story they like to tell begins when Liliana makes a university dean dance the tango.

Liliana leads. She holds the dean firmly in her arms and brings her lips as close to his as she can without kissing him. The dean pants like a puppy. To scotch rumors that he's her lover she says, "If dancing the tango gets him that hot, he'd die in bed. And he's not dead, so he's not my lover." Before the remark can lose its sting, word gets out that el *Pato* has a heart attack during a night with Liliana. And according to at least one anecdote, a fling with Liliana costs a man his life. I've always thought I may have provided grist for that mill because on two separate occasions I was hospitalized after her brother Rubén beat me up: the first time for taking her on trips with me; the second for sleeping with her. I can say from experience that Liliana is dangerous as well as beautiful. Courting the danger excites me.

In the San Rafael district, where the Montoya family has lived for many years, residents cling to a memory that also remains fresh with the Olivares generation.

Liliana is twelve, and she's watching a game of street soccer from the sidewalk. A kid scores a goal. He grabs the ball and lays it at Liliana's feet as a tribute. A youngster from the opposing side tries to retrieve the ball so the game can continue. But the adversary who laid it at Liliana's feet collars him and knocks him down. The blow leaves him writhing on the ground fighting for breath. His teammates rush to avenge him. A pitched battle breaks out to the horror of neighbors who see it from their windows. The incident leads to an Iliad of street fights that plague San Rafael long after the soccer game on Tamarindo—a side street that may have been renamed—is forgotten.

These chronic skirmishes remind the Olivares generation of the strife between the two American football teams el *Pato* fields at the university. He wants to make Liliana the mascot for both sides, but when the captain of one intramural team takes her by the hand, the captain of the other tells him to let go of her. The whole student body is swept up in the ensuing brawl, and it takes el *Pato* days to restore peace within the university walls.

A dust-up in a dancehall called Jacarandas also becomes legend. Liliana emerges from the restroom complaining that someone just tried to feel her up. El *Pato* has yet to arrive at the time of the incident; in his place Olivares is playing host and overseeing the bevy of coeds he brought along for the occasion. When Liliana tells the old man what happened, he deploys the skill to which he owes his success in life: duck and do nothing. When el *Pato* arrives and hears of the affront to Liliana, the man who accosted her is at the next table and is besieging her with suggestive looks and gestures. El *Pato* rises from his chair and, flinging caution to the wind, upends the neighbor's table onto his lap. The outburst wins el *Pato* a trip to the police station where he gains the upper hand with a phone call to an influential friend.

El *Pato* also stars in a memorable bar fight at the Buca Bar on Bucareli Street when he singlehandedly takes on a band of toughs that invade the Buca like tourists on their first trip to the French Riviera. These interlopers from the nearby Guerrero district see Liliana dancing with el *Pato*, and one of them tries to cut in while another gropes her. El *Pato* snatches a bottle from a table, breaks it over the groper's head, and waves the jagged edge at his pals like a glass trident. The toughs pull switchblades from under their belts. A dance of thrusts and parries lasts until a phalanx of waiters entangles the aroused combatants in tablecloths while shouting at them to cease and desist. Whenever I hear this story I have to admit that el *Pato* put his life on the line in a way that I probably wouldn't have.

There is, on the other hand, the day I eat with Liliana at La Cava, a restaurant near the University campus on the south edge of the city. She's only been el *Pato's* girl for a few months, but she's already flush with credit cards and crisp new bills in high denominations in a brand new purse. She pays with a flourish and says we must come back soon for another meal on her bill. She intends to visit the ladies' room before we leave, but a drunk gets up from his table and blocks her path. He won't let her by unless she kisses him first. I pick up a chair and bash it over his head. The blow leaves him facedown in a debris field of splintered chair parts with the cushion on his back like a saddle. His friends gang-tackle me, and once again the waiters intervene. At the police station we swap insults until I'm allowed to phone my newspaper and the editor invokes my immunity as a journalist.

This scene reminds me of another which I know circulates behind my back and always draws a snicker from listeners. Embellished by legend, the episode presents a would-be writer who becomes an honorary member of the Montoya family. Liliana quickly learns she can lead him around by the nose. The writer's favorite pastimes are drinking with Liliana and incurring the wrath of her brother Rubén, who finds his sister and the writer naked in the bathroom of their house. Rubén administers a beating so ferocious that it puts the writer in the hospital. That same day Liliana comes home from her first party with the

Olivares generation. She dances and sings for this assemblage of aging plodders who never forget the occasion and fondly embellish the events of that day. Liliana climbs on a table and begins to strip only to be dragged off by el *Pato* in medias res. A short time later, having stilled his amorous pawings, she's back on the table to conclude a performance which proves to many of the onlookers that she's insatiable.

A political scientist who drools for her concludes that Liliana triggers the "Hobbes effect" in men. She reduces them to to their primal state and turns them into violent and primitive—but passionate—lovers. It makes them immune to danger, unable to resist the thrill of the chase and capture of the woman of their heart's desire.

From her knees to her hips Liliana tingles with a low flame that never goes out. She has bright eyes and the slender waist of a girl; her stomach ripples as she breathes. She has smooth skin, a long neck, small hands, and fingernails she bites to the quick. If she lets it grow, her hair falls straight and uncurled to her shoulders. She has almond eyes and when her thin lips part—to order from a menu, for example—the forward thrust of her white teeth show she intends to have her way.

None of this has a thing to do with her irresistible beauty. Except that I'm not alone; it's irresistible to other men, too. But only Liliana makes me wonder how beauty is passed out. It confers unasked-for benefits and, often, great anguish on its possessors, turning them into self-defeating trophies for others to covet. In recent years I've thought a lot about the kind of love that makes a man like el *Pato* Vértiz a slave to a woman twenty years his junior. Though it repels me, I can't help wondering what traps a relatively older man in such an arid and submissive relationship, that makes him capable of satisfying such insane demands as to find a hitman to avenge his lover's little sister. Which is what el *Pato* does: he finds a professional killer. In the third telling of her story Liliana says: "I never respected him after that because he didn't take care of me. He shouldn't have let me murder someone."

There's only one difference between el *Pato* and me: el *Pato* fell into Liliana's trap and paid the price. I didn't; I didn't win her over either.

M Y SEARCH FOR LILIANA must proceed with no help from her family. In many ways my estrangement from the Montoyas is my own fault, a hidden cost of my pursuit of Liliana. My friend Rubén Montoya throws me out of the house after finding Liliana with me in the bathroom with her skirt up and her panties around her ankles. My shoes are a disaster, and to this day I'm mortified whenever I think of how disgraceful my dirty, unlaced shoes must have looked at the time. Rubén hounds me out of the bathroom and the house under a barrage of punches. What I've done is unspeakable to him. When he hears Liliana's involved with el *Pato* Vértiz, he kicks her out too and blames me for abusing his sister and making her vulnerable to the likes of el *Pato*. Rubén will always remember me as the first stepping stone on Liliana's downward path. The first male to overstep her boundaries. When I run into him in a bookstore, I fully expect he'll attack me, but he only nods. I misread his gesture and think he's offering to make amends. I ask how he's doing.

"Fine," he says.

I ask about Liliana.

"I don't know," he replies. "I put her out of my life the same as you."

That's when I see the cold hatred in his eyes, the indelible hurt inflicted by my incest.

Rubén Montoya starts getting into fights over his

sister at an early age, and he keeps fighting until he's old enough to understand he can't hold on to her. It's a lesson that's pounded into him during an after-school fight with a classmate who, if he wanted to, could have smashed Rubén's face in and broken his ribs. Kids who know what's about to happen gather for a no-holds-barred test of masculinity in a small roundabout where several streets intersect. His rival's first moves tell Rubén he can't win. The other boy has honed his fighting skills by challenging and defeating anyone who dares meet him in the roundabout.

For Rubén the ordeal marks the day when he stops being a child and becomes an adult. He's suddenly gripped by a sense of his own mortality: the kid he's agreed to fight could kill him. He absorbs the first punch in the mouth without flinching, the second one hits him in the temple and makes his head ring, the third gets him in the Adam's apple and takes his breath away. More blows connect with merciless precision. As soon as Rubén's knocked down, the other boy is on top of him, straddling him, ready to pound his face into the gravel. Then something unexpected happens. The other boy pulls a punch that could have knocked Rubén's teeth out or cracked his head open. Barely an inch from his face, the punch becomes a feint. Before he can get up, the other boy aims but chooses not to land a kick in Rubén's exposed ribs as he lies sobbing and defenseless in the dirt.

Onlookers help Rubén to his feet. He sees Liliana watching him from the sidewalk, and her presence compounds his misery. His other sister Dorotea steps forward with friends to help him home. Being cared for by girls younger than he is makes him feel small, less of a grownup. They keep him from stumbling on the way to his house, then settle him into an overstuffed easy chair near the door. Liliana appears with a washbasin and hot water. Rubén never forgets what she tells him while bathing his wounds. She's angry at the boy who beat him up, she told him not to pick a fight with her brother; Rubén's always harassing her admirers, she says, but he doesn't speak for her. Liliana can speak for herself.

Rubén is bruised and disgraced. His body looks terrible, but it's nothing compared to the look of despair on his battered face when Liliana lifts his swollen cheeks between her hands and looks him in the eye. She snuffs out his youth by saying, "I like him, Rubén, but now I won't go near him because of what he did to you. But I do like him. The same way I like other boys. Can you forgive me for liking other boys? I like lots of boys, and I like them a lot."

This is how Rubén learns he can't hold on to his sister. Liliana is thirteen at the time.

It's been a while since I've heard anything about the Montoya tribe. Chance helps fill the gap on a trip to the dentist. In his waiting room I read a story about honors awarded to adolescents who have overcome handicaps. One of the honorees is Dorotea's son. He appears with his parents in an accompanying photo. His name is Arturo Heisler Montoya. He looks tall and frail. The thick glasses he wears to correct his nearsightedness exaggerate the size of his sad eyes.

This gangling youth is an extravagantly talented mathematician who was considered mentally retarded as a child. His father, Arno Heisler Gotze, though born in Mexico, is the head of a German pharmaceutical firm. His mother, Dorotea Montoya Giner, is the good fairy who fights for her son against all odds, the embattled parent who sees genius where teachers and doctors have seen only autism or an unusual variant of Down syndrome. Dorotea is the same height as her husband in the picture, but neither is as tall as their son. He has broad shoulders, long arms, and a wide forehead. His ears stick out from beneath a head of carefully combed black hair, and he's looking straight into the camera. He in no way resembles el *Catracho*.

I think of Dorotea's son as a shining anomaly. It must be like having a beautiful monster in the house. I draw on my wiles as a writer and attempt to learn more about the Heisler Montoyas from the organization that awarded the prize. They withhold the family's home address, but they do give me a phone number. Dorotea answers my first call. I hang up without speaking. A week later I call again. The maid answers. I ask to speak with the lady of the house, and the maid asks who's calling. I give her my name and tell her why I called after so many years. This gives Dorotea the opportunity to refuse or accept my request to see her. Her voice sounds clear and pleased when she answers.

"Serrano, what an honor. To what do I owe this distinction?"

To the honors given her son, I say. I tell her about the magazine in the dentist's office and the article with the photo.

"You're a bad boy, Serrano. You disappeared without even saying goodbye to us."

I said my farewells to Rubén, I tell her.

"But not to us, Serrano. Are you coming to see me?"

I tell her that's why I called. She gives me an address, a day, and a time.

On the day of her choice I arrive at the appointed mid-morning hour. She lives in an enormous house in one of the city's finest neighborhoods. I can see woods to the north of the house. Dorotea invites me to be seated on one of the white leather sofas in the sala. She's no longer the young woman I remember, she's an elegant matron now. But the young girl still shows through when she says something that makes her laugh or when, for some unknowable reason, her eyes suddenly light up. There are frown lines on her forehead.

She has me repeat my story about the magazine, the diploma, and my dentist's waiting room. I compliment her on her son. She nods and smiles. She's dedicated herself to rescuing him from a world that doesn't understand him, she says. Saving her son saved her faith. I ask if she's a believer.

"I'm my own church."

Her words don't make sense. There's no room for believers or churches in the Montoya family. Genes and the Jacobin library of Dr. Montoya, their unbelieving progenitor, explain everything.

"I have plenty to say to you but nothing for us to chat about. I shouldn't even be seeing you after what you did to my sister."

I tell her I didn't do a thing to her sister.

"You didn't rescue her, Serrano. That's what you did to her. You didn't stand by her."

I tell her Liliana had no use for me, which is a lie to which I add a grain of truth: Liliana frightens me.

"But you're here looking for her," Dorotea says.

"Why did you come if you weren't trying to find her?"

Rather than answer, I ask how she's been.

"See?" she says. "Don't you see? You came here because you're looking for her. Because you need to talk about her. About el *Pato* and all that. But I don't want to talk about it."

What she calls it is exactly what she talks about except here it is different from mine. Here it is the love between el *Pato* and Liliana. She's strangely elated as she warms to her subject.

"I think they were happy until my sister lost her first baby. When she lost the second one, it was all over. She couldn't even look el *Pato* in the eye after that. Didn't she tell you? Never? She was a fool, it would have been good for her. Thinking about you made her feel better, she always said you and she were unfinished business. The two of you. For each other. That when all else was lost, you remained. But you left her, Serrano. And she let you go. How dumb. I'd never have let go of you."

I ask if I heard her right, that Liliana lost a baby.

"Two."

I ask when.

"When she was with el *Pato*. In the second month of her first pregnancy. The second was in the fourth month, and it went very badly. Nothing can be done for her now."

I ask if they were miscarriages or abortions.

"Don't be offensive, Serrano. Nobody in my family would do a thing like that."

I ask what she means by "nothing can be done."

"She can't have children. She tried but couldn't. Now she'll never be able to have a child."

I finally ask where Liliana is.

"I don't know. I have no idea." Her eyes fill with tears. Dorotea's grief is touching. But her tears irritate me.

I suggest we talk about el *Catracho*.

"El *Catracho*?"

Your friend el *Catracho*, I remind her.

"I don't have a friend el *Catracho*, Serrano. What does *Catracho* mean anyway?"

I say it's another word for Honduran, like Aztec for Mexican. Can she tell me about el *Catracho*, her Honduran boyfriend?

She laughs in my face.

"What boyfriend, Serrano? I don't have boyfriends, I'm a married woman."

Her teenage boyfriend, I insist. El *Catracho*.

"I didn't have boyfriends in my teens. What are you talking about, Serrano? I had my first boyfriend when I was twenty, and now he's my husband. What have you been smoking?"

I know all about el *Catracho*, I tell her. I have all the details. The date, the police file, the version written up by the agent assigned to the case.

"What case, Serrano? What date? What agent?"

I drop the subject. I realize the visit has ended in the worst possible way, but Dorotea prolongs it insufferably. She wants to show me around the house. And show me she does. On the ground floor there's the sala where we talk, then another sala, then a dining room and the kitchen with a butler's pantry in between. The dining room overlooks a studio with books from floor to ceiling. Arno's studio, she explains. Inside the studio he has a folding screen from India. The kitchen opens onto a terrace. Between the terrace and the yard is a swimming pool. Beyond the yard a woods. We cross the yard. Near the edge of the woods is a stable, an exercise ring, and a guest cottage. Dorotea's son rides every day on a horse named Perelman. She escorts me around the premises and tells me all about her house one thing at a time like a tour guide. On the walk back to the house we talk about her gifted son. He's her life. Though she never met her father, she's sure there's something of Dr. Montoya in her son. We come to the door. She thanks me for visiting. She blinks when she extends her hand in farewell. Before she shuts the door, she blinks again. And she blinks in my memory.

That night I have a dream about Dorotea that I record in my notebooks. "I see Dorotea walk into a grimy bar and come out with a grimy young man who takes her to a grimy hotel from which she emerges with fresh makeup and goes home."

*F*ELO FERNÁNDEZ CALLS and wants to know what Comandante Neri and I talked about. I say a police case I'm considering turning into a novel. He tells me Neri went to see el *Pato* Vértiz. Neri told el *Pato* he'd been talking to me and asked for money. *Felo* wants to know what I talked about with Neri.

I refuse to tell him. The story of el *Catracho* is a secret between Liliana and me (and el *Pato* and Dorotea). I'm clearly not a trustworthy keeper of the secret. I've left *Felo* vulnerable to at least two more people, Antúnez and Neri. Antúnez owns Neri. Neri must have told Antúnez what he spoke about with me. They both must have wondered why this case mattered to me and raised their antennas. Neri is a policeman who smells money in unsolved enigmas; Antúnez a politician who smells human misery he can exploit. I ponder this while *Felo* speaks of the generational clash that makes Antúnez hate el *Pato* with a passion. While visiting el *Pato*, Neri mentions that Antúnez put him in contact with me. El *Pato* fears Antúnez is up to something and Neri is his emissary. When *Felo* says this, I realize I've squeezed out too much toothpaste and can't get it back in the tube. I'm faced with what great strategists have always called "unintended consequences": wanting to bomb a weapons factory, you also hit a school full of children; trying to make a fat woman slender, you turn her into a suicidal anorexic. By investigating the death of el

Catracho, I rekindle the interest of an extortionist cop and a politician in a cold case. The politician hates el *Pato* as much as I do, but he wants to make sure his hatred has consequences.

El *Pato* is frantic, *Felo* says. He wants to know what Neri told me and what I told Neri. I gather el *Pato* has kept our big secret about el *Catracho* from *Felo*, and *Felo* hasn't told el *Pato* he introduced me to Antúnez.

In this regard *Felo* says, "I made a big mistake getting you together with Antúnez, boss. He used to be friends with el *Pato*, but the friendship turned to hate of the worst kind. Antúnez got his start in politics from el *Pato*, then he leapfrogged him into a job el *Pato* wanted for himself. I thought this was water under the bridge, but it wasn't. It ran deeper than I thought. I'm not asking you to help me deal with that. But could you help me clear the air a bit with el *Pato*? I know how much you despise him, and you're not alone. But el *Pato* is a shadow of his former self. He couldn't possibly be worse off. He's a Job without a god. A disaster."

What *Felo* says pleases me but doesn't convince me. The obscene thought of seeing for myself how far el *Pato* Vértiz has fallen is what convinces me. Call it seepage from a sour disposition: a sour disposition that basks in someone else's misery.

I agree to meet el *Pato* at Sanborn's on San Antonio Street, near my house. As he enters, he shoots glances to his sides and behind him as if he thinks he's being followed. I described el *Pato* already: his teeth are yellow; his nose is flat; his bald spot opens on a pale scalp with black freckles; his shoulders are stooped; and he has a gut as big as a seven-month baby bulge.

In his hand is a book of mine he just bought that's still wrapped in plastic. He wants me to write a dedication to the memory of good times past. I don't remember any good times with him, so I sign it in memory of good times. By which I mean now when he looks a wreck. If Antúnez were here, he'd be enjoying this. I'm not Antúnez, but I'm enjoying it anyway. Then the conversation begins.

I start by apologizing for having attracted the attention of Neri and Antúnez to "our business." "Our business" is my proposed shorthand for the murder of el *Catracho*. I tell him about my meeting with Neri, about the questions I asked, not Neri's recollection of the murder. I say that when I spoke to Neri, his memory of whoever it was that took the girl to see the body was unclear. I say Neri may have tried to remember, but the only thing that stuck in his mind was asking the man for money in memory of good times.

"There was nothing for Neri to remember," el *Pato* tells me. "I remember what happened perfectly."

His words break through my condescension. I ask if he knew Neri.

"For years. I had to pay him off regularly."

I'm taken aback, and there's no concealing my surprise from el *Pato*. He's the one who's condescending now.

"I'm going to tell you something, mister writer. I'm going to tell you what I know about 'our business.' Are you willing to listen?"

I nod, disconcerted. Is his odd way of addressing me—of calling me "mister writer"—meant to put me in my place? Suddenly el *Pato*'s in control, and I'm not.

"First of all, mister writer, I didn't order anything concerning 'our business.' I got an absurd order from Liliana which I ignored at first rather than start an argument. Later I did things to avoid an argument. As the saying goes, it's better to promise than regret. Or something like that. I knew people in city government. The prosecutor, may he rest in peace, was a friend of mine. He gave Antúnez, who was one of my best students, a job in his office. So I asked Antúnez to do something for me and to make it appear he was acting on his own behalf. I had him look into the alleged doings of el *Catracho* to see if there was any truth—never mind the whole truth—in the details Liliana gave me. They were all quite vague except for the address of the cathouse that was right where Liliana said it was in the San Rafael district. Antúnez asked what I expected to find in such a place, and I made the mistake of telling him it was personal, that it had to do with smears against a family looking for revenge. He deliberately misunderstood me. Among other things, he decided that by not asking him to do something, I was implicitly asking him to do it. I just wanted him to investigate, nothing more. A month later I asked what, if anything, he'd learned. I just asked the question, I didn't ask him to do anything. He said el *Catracho* had been killed that same evening. 'Mission accomplished,' he said and asked for further instructions. 'There are no instructions, Antúnez, I didn't give you instructions.' 'You did tacitly,' the bastard said. 'Tacitly, my ass,' I said. 'What did you do, motherfucker?' Because he's the one who gave the order to kill el *Catracho*. He had someone bring me the photos to calm me down. Or to drive me crazy. I took them to Liliana that same night."

He pauses theatrically. I ask how she reacted to the photos.

"Tears of anger welled up in her eyes."

I ask if Liliana believed him.

He stutters as he says, "She believed me."

I ask if she wanted him to take her to see the body even though she believed him.

"No, mister writer. Are you crazy? Who told you that?"

I tell him Liliana did.

"Was she drunk? Drunk she'd say that and a whole lot more. She went so far as to say she supervised the execution. Pure bullshit, mister writer, don't pay any attention to it. It's not what happened."

He sips his coffee and gulps like a turkey to get it down. Before continuing, he resettles himself in his chair. "Liliana lies, mister writer. Our Liliana was a liar. She'd have killed to be a femme fatale, to be seen as a great lady Why do you think she got involved with me? But it didn't happen. Our relationship was simpler than that, very basic. I got her out of her house, gave her money, showed her the world, then she got tired of me and went her own way. If only we'd planned a killing together, a murder born of our complicity, of our love, then I'd never have let her go. She'd still be my prisoner. You see, Liliana was the best thing that ever happened to me."

El *Pato* reaches into his back pocket and pulls out a billfold with more layers than a palimpsest. From a hidden compartment he extracts a photo secreted under slips of onion paper. He shows me a faded black and white photo of Liliana with her arms around him.

He's looking straight into the camera, smiling and fulfilled. She's kissing his ear like a great tennis player kissing her trophy at Wimbledon.

"This is how she was with me while we were together," el *Pato* says. "Just look how happy I am. You can see it in my face." He's the picture of contentment in the photo. "That's the way it was while it lasted, and that's how it still is for me. The photo says it all. So stop looking for cards up someone's sleeve, mister writer."

El *Pato* has a knack for mangling cliches, but he's no match for *Felo* Fernández, who's the reigning master of garble. ("Power makes fools of intelligent men, boss, and it drives idiots out of their minds.")

I ask el *Pato* how Neri fits in the picture he paints.

"Neri was my guide on this sad adventure. He took me to see el *Catracho* the night he was killed." Once again I ask if Liliana went with him.

"I already told you Liliana lies, mister writer. She likes to make herself seem more important than she is."

I let the question of Liliana ride. I ask if he saw el *Catracho*'s body in the cathouse that night.

"I didn't have the stomach to look at it, but I was there preferred by Neri and Antúnez." He says "preferred," but he means protected.

I ask if the Neri he's talking about is the Neri I know.

"The same one," el *Pato* says. "And the same Antúnez, the bastard who sent Neri to see me. By then he was my enemy, mister writer. That asshole Antúnez was my mimesis." (He means nemesis.) "And that motherfucker Neri took photos that he later used to blackmail me."

I don't believe half of what el *Pato* says. Moreover, I don't believe his major premise. I think failure and misfortune caused him to regret it, but what he says makes what he did quite clear. He doesn't give Antúnez specific instructions, but he does tell him to be sure to act in a way that will give el *Pato* deniability if things go wrong. What follows—the dilemma and the enigma contained in this story—is not so clear. There are two possibilities.

One: Antúnez does el *Pato's* bidding; he kills el *Catracho* and lets el *Pato* know he's followed orders. Then, to make sure there are witnesses, he has Neri escort el *Pato* and a companion to the scene of the crime and take pictures.

Two: Antúnez doesn't do as he's told by el *Pato*. But he happens to have on his desk the report on a dead man whose remains could very well be el *Catracho's*. He uses this corpse as a stand-in for el *Catracho's* and tells el *Pato* mission accomplished. He makes sure there are witnesses to testify that el *Pato* arranged the hit through Neri, a rookie cop who escorts el *Pato* and his companion to the scene of the crime and takes pictures of them looking at the cadaver.

Either hypothesis changes the plot and makes el *Pato* beholden to Antúnez. A time will come when the former student makes his old teacher pay. Instead of a seeker of vengeance for his girlfriend's dishonored sister, el *Pato* becomes a puppet whose strings are pulled by Antúnez.

What interests me about el *Pato's* version isn't his self-exoneration but the anguish that comes over him as he speaks of that dark moment. El *Pato's* claim that what happened wasn't his fault strikes me less as an attempt to escape blame than the frustration of a petty tyrant whose lover walked out on him. In the throes of amorous desperation he wants to prove he's the strong, decisive man he says he is. But he isn't. The confidences he purports to share in Sanborn's reveal that he's devastated, not elated, when he tries to think of himself as the coolheaded instigator of a murder. His passion for Liliana drives him to suggest that the punishment for a crime that he's not up to committing himself should be execution. He's a garden variety rogue, a spoiler who thinks he can issue a license to kill. But he can't. Like Macbeth he drowns in the moral depths of a deeply immoral man; homicide robs him of his sleep. For his accomplice, the truly soulless Antúnez, life goes on.

I think I can make el *Pato's* life easier by telling him what Neri told me: that Antúnez sold him on a false execution. El *Catracho* happened to be killed because he was found in the wrong place at the wrong time, not on the strength of el *Pato's* request to Antúnez, his favorite and his protégé, his mimesis and his nemesis. El *Catracho* died because a band of rogue cops tried to get rid of witnesses and clean up after themselves following a murder that could get them in trouble. But I don't tell him anything. If this knowledge can take a load off anyone's mind, I don't want it to be el *Pato's*.

I spend several days going over books and chronicles about an ugly period in Mexico City that I'd rather forget, a time of well-documented police corruption, brutality and misconduct. When law enforcement went rogue, anthropologists, historians and concerned citizens took note. They were outraged by a justice system that relied on summary executions to keep order, that bent to the will of influential people who liked having their grudges settled in the cells of their precinct station house. I soon abandon this research. It suffices to convince me Neri's version of events is closer to the truth than el *Pato's*; it's simpler and more in tune with the era. El *Catracho* just happened to be in the way at the start of a hunt for bigger game.

DOROTEA IS THE YOUNGEST of the Montoyas. The oldest is Ángel, who was born in 1940 and is a doctor like his father. The second is Matilde, 1941, a nurse like her mother. The third is Arcelia, 1942, who dies in infancy. The fourth is the second Arcelia, 1943, who replaces the deceased Arcelia. The fifth is Antonio, 1945, who is mentally retarded. The sixth is Regina, 1946, who has had two good marriages. The seventh is Margarita, 1948, who dies in childhood. The eighth is Sigifredo, 1950, a chemist who emigrates to Cologne. The ninth is my friend Rubén, 1952, who has made a career for himself in theater. The tenth is Ricardo, 1954, Liliana's twin who dies on a pilgrimage to Chalma. The eleventh is Liliana, the leading lady of this story. The twelfth is Teodoro, 1955, who becomes an anthropologist and lives among the Mazateco Indians. Five years go by in the Montoya family before Margarita, the thirteenth sibling is born in 1960 and replaces the deceased Margarita, then comes number fourteen: Dorotea, 1961, who also has a role in this story. When Dorotea is two, her father, Dr. Montoya, dies of a stroke. Liliana is nine; Rubén and I are both eleven.

I don't actually make a firm decision; I simply hear myself telling *Felo* Fernández I need someone to investigate Dorotea. He has a business card sent to me that says:

Investigations 360
Malaquías (Eye of God)

The 360 suggests the peripheral vision of an owl, the ability to spy in all directions in all media: physical surveillance; phone taps; online espionage; indoor and outdoor videotaping at home or at work.

"How much espionage do you want?" he asks.

I reply, "How many kinds of espionage are there?"

Question:

Is what you want to know indoors or outdoors?

I'm charmed by his use of know. The word indoors unnerves me. I'm a spy with a conscience; I say outdoors only.

Question:

Surveillance?

I agree to surveillance.

Photo or video surveillance?

I agree to photo and video.

Phone taps?

Phone taps, no. I cringe at phone taps. I'm a spy with scruples.

Particular activities or places?

I'm forced to admit it's not really Dorotea I'm looking for but her sister.

Name of the sister?

When Malaquías finishes grilling me about what I'm looking for, I realize I've learned plenty from Dorotea without acquiring the crumb of information needed to discover Liliana's whereabouts. That's what I want Malaquías to find. I want him to do for me what I've put off doing on my own. I can't bring myself to tell him in so many words that all I really care about is finding Liliana.

Felo Fernández has told me Malaquías is a novice in his trade and can be expected to make the mistakes novices make. But, as *Felo* readily admits, he doesn't know another more seasoned Malaquías. Malaquías's espionage know-how is largely confined to surveillance. As he's the first to tell me, his phone taps leave much to be desired. Curiously, his confession of professional weakness strengthens my confidence in him. I'm not hiring him to do phone taps.

Malaquías pays me no mind. He taps Dorotea's phone anyway and learns that Liliana calls her once a week. I scold him, I curse him, I nearly hit him when he tells me this, but I agree to listen to his clandestine recording. The conversation takes place days after I visit Dorotea. On the phone she says:

"Your old boyfriend came by to stir up trouble."

Something that sounds breathtakingly like Liliana's voice comes from the other end of the line.

"He was bound to return."

Malaquías asks me if I recognize that voice as the voice of the person I'm searching for, Liliana Montoya. I say yes. He asks if I want to save the tape. I didn't order it, but he'll let me have it at no extra cost. Once again I agree. He asks if I want him to keep on recording the phone calls. I restate my scruple about espionage and tell him no.

Malaquías's cassette preserves this dialogue:

"Your old squeeze is back to haunt you."

"Which one?"

"The usual one."

"How sweet. I knew he'd be back. How is he?"

"Old and scrawny."

"The poor man. When did he come?"

"Three weeks ago."

"Why didn't you tell me?"

"This is the fifth time I've told you. Why don't you take notes?"

"I hate taking notes. When are you coming?"

"Next month."

"Are you bringing what we agreed you would?"

"What we spoke about is forbidden."

"Don't worry about what's forbidden, Dorotea. The people here are crazy, they think I'm crazy."

The recorded call links Dorotea's cell phone to the psychiatric ward at Sanatorio Miranda, the hospital where they think Liliana is crazy. It takes me a month of foot-dragging and three separate attempts to reach the counter in the psychiatric ward. When I say "attempt" I mean I pull into the hospital parking lot three times only to change my mind about going inside. I finally take the plunge. Looking after the ward is a small, childlike blonde whose eyes sparkle as if they hide a secret. It seems to me she knows who I am, why I've come, and all the lies I'm prepared to tell.

I like hospitals that still have open spaces with trees. At Sanatorio Miranda there are eucalyptus, big lawns and walkways between the buildings for each specialty. Large cats lie in the dust, napping in the sun.

I don't know of another hospital with cats. Here they do their duty hunting rats and vermin. Let's not talk about birds. I have mixed feelings about cats; I envy their self-assurance and steady gaze. If I had these traits, I could do without stuttering what I now do with stuttering. I ask about patient Montoya at the counter and say I'm her relative. I'd like to be able to lick my whiskers and stare at the cheerful little blonde whose luminous aquamarine eyes look up at me over the tortoiseshell frames of her glasses. She says my patient's in Patio One and asks if I know the way. Without waiting for an answer she says I should go back the way I came and go left on the red brick walkway marked Patio One to a door where there's a counter like hers. I should repeat my request to the girl there.

I retrace my footsteps to the Patio One sign, which I recall seeing on my way in. The sign has an arrow pointing to a path that runs along a walkway next to a wall which gives way to a chain-link fence. The fence ends at a high brick wall with squat towers like sentry boxes at the edge of the hospital grounds. There's no gate where I am, but through the rhomboidal chinks in the fence I see withered gardens and a maze of S-shaped cement walks. Sunning themselves or strolling about the compound, some without but most with their nurses, are the blissed-out patients of the psychiatric ward. Some paths bend towards the area for patients in wheelchairs. I think I see Liliana in one of them accompanied by a nurse with large breasts and an expressionless face. Liliana is staring at the wall surrounding the hospital. Her hair falls to her shoulders, and a light breeze ripples a wisp of hair over her forehead. Her nose is straight and sharp, her cheeks pale, her forehead broadened by thinning hair or a breath of wind that lifts the loose bangs off her temple. Her back is as straight as the back of the wheelchair she's sitting in, her neck and spine athletically upright, unhindered by the wheelchair's restraints. Her thighs and knees are round and firm under her white hospital gown. Her brown calves are smooth, freshly bathed and moisturized, and I feel a tremor of arousal at the sight of her bare skin. At just this moment Liliana, as if drawn by a surge of electricity, looks at the spot in the fence where I'm standing. Her head bobs like a startled bird. She flaps a hand in my direction like the fin of a seal and says, "Is that you?"

Of course it is, but I'm not sure who she is. More to the point, how can anyone be sure who we are as we gesture at each other across the fifty feet that separate the path where Liliana is from the chain-link fence where I am?

Strange thoughts course through my head. Her fettered wave reminds me of the wife of one of el *Pato* Vértiz's successors. Upon hearing that her husband is involved with Liliana, the crazed woman throws herself off a rock not far from where the cliff divers of La Quebrada perform in Acapulco. A different version of the tale has her leap from the heights of a roller-coaster in the Chapultepec amusement park. In a more literary account she meets her demise by defenestrating herself from a flat in the Nonoalco Tlatelolco apartment complex onto the railroad tracks near where Ixca Cienfuegos says "This is where we're fated to live" in the Carlos Fuentes novel.

I go back the way I came to the counter where the doll-like blonde holds forth. She gives me new directions that lead me inside the wire at Patio One. I follow the path to where Liliana is. First, I see her firm thighs under her gown and her silken skin from the knees down. Then I see her feet are bare. They have high arches, thick ankles and yellow soles. The flat nail of her big toe sports a radiant coat of cherry red enamel. Her painted big toe fills me with a near fatal urge to kiss her.

I station myself in front of her and look her in the eye. She returns my stare and smiles as if pleased by an effort that produced the desired result. Age and illness—or the ministrations of her doctors—have sharpened her features. The pills she takes make her eat less, sleep more, and want for nothing. Chemically speaking, she's cured: pleasantly resigned to the here and now on a regimen that keeps her placid as a cow.

What can I say? To my eyes she's more beautiful than ever. A bit subdued, lacking the old spark, but in its absence is a cloudless smile, a youthful glow, the edenic beauty of a face neither disfigured nor enhanced by experience. She's more beautiful and less desirable than ever. Neutral, pure, abstractly beautiful. Also: sedated, ethereal, starved of conflict or desire. Her eyes are glazed and empty as if her corneas had been hardened. Even in this state, the faint light that escapes her glassy stare is touching, her serenity the shriveled fruit of despair.

I'm reminded, as I'm often reminded, of the first time I saw Liliana on the arm of el *Pato* Vértiz at the university. Her face had yet to lose its now restored freshness. Seeing her arm in arm with el *Pato* made my blood boil with brotherly rage as if I'd seen my sister selling herself on a street corner, drunk and plastered with makeup. But on that day with el *Pato* Liliana isn't drunk, and she's wearing little makeup. She's dazzling. Strolling with el *Pato*, she's well-groomed and well-dressed, as poised, proud and deferential as a young bride under the spell of a phlegmatic spouse. What overcomes me isn't brotherly rage, it's the spite of a jilted rival. The scene ends when I make up my mind to drop her. I'm the one who will let her go, who doesn't care if she ends up in the arms of el *Pato* Vértiz. I'm not brave enough or careless enough to cast my lot with her. I don't share her thirst for adventure, and glitz doesn't impress me. I'm in no hurry to slough off the skin I was born in.

I remember the days I spent running away from the schoolyard bully who beat me up whenever he saw me. I ran from him for a whole year, then I quit running, and he stopped beating me up. I resolve to stop chasing Liliana Montoya.

When Liliana sees me approach, she tells the nurse to leave us alone. The nurse steps away. Lilliana doesn't get out of her wheelchair. Instead, she tells me to come closer. She puts her face next to mine and says:

"Get me out of here, Serrano."

Her cheek is cold under a veil of sweat. She places her hand on the back of my neck and pulls me closer. Then she sniffs the skin between my shirt collar and my ear. She sniffs down my shirt towards my chest. She smells my armpit under my jacket. Her conclusion is: "You've gone out of your way to avoid me. Avoiding me is all you care about."

She gets out of her wheelchair, takes my hand, and starts walking. We stroll around Patio One.

"I could tell you I know this patio by heart, Serrano. But I don't. Nothing in this patio is worth learning by heart."

She's stopped calling me Serranito. She's stopped being what she is too.

"What would you like to know about me, Serrano? I won't hide anything from you."

I learn that el *Pato* Vértiz comes to see her but doesn't tell *Felo* Fernández. Dorotea also visits but declined to tell me. Liliana tells me they're ashamed, ashamed of her illness. I ask her to explain.

"I turn on and off, Serrano. I go from heaven to hell. To get better I'm supposed to float somewhere between the two, but there isn't any in-between. Here, where you see me now, I'm in the middle of nowhere."

As I said, she looks splendid to me. Fresh, recovered. As usual, the sun on the high plain is fierce, and she knits her brow when she turns to look at me. But neither the sun nor her furrowed brow casts any shadow that darkens her expression or hardens the look in her eyes. As I already suggested, they retain an unquenchable flicker of despair. In another face this flicker might be anguish; in Liliana's it's adorable.

In sum, her illness is chronic and cyclical; pills stabilize her and keep her in the state she's in now.

"I'm off my game, Serrano. I'm tediously healthy. Which is pure tedium. I'm only healthy if I'm bored. For me it's life with no flavor. It's just happy boredom. No pain, no anguish. No urges either. No parties. Nothing inside me that wants to party. I'm now the woman you love but not the woman who loves you because she's the crazy one, Serrano. Right now I remember you as just a brother. You see how sad that is?"

She tells me she's been in this psychiatric ward three times since our last meeting four years ago. The first time was shortly after our missed connection on the day my book about Huitzilac was released. Her reason for not waiting for me lacks the ring of truth.

"It made me mad to feel you so far away from me, Serrano. It made me cry, and I couldn't stop sobbing. I kept telling myself he'll humiliate me, he's going to brush me off, and this time he should. Because you'd changed, Serrano. You weren't my Serranito anymore, you were Serrano now. To tell the truth, I was afraid of you."

Her chatter leaves me cold, and my silence speaks volumes. She finishes her explanation. "I needed a drink badly. I went to get one at the bar in the hotel while you were signing books. I woke up three days later at Dorotea's house. Asking for you."

My silence still resonates.

"Don't hate me, Serrano. Get me out of here."

MY NOTEBOOKS SAY THE DATE when I find Liliana on the grounds of her hospital is November 4, 1999. I visit her at least once a week from then on. She clings to me and whispers in my ear:

"Get me out of here."

I can get her out. There really isn't anything holding her back. She's on a strict schedule of medications, but she can come and go from the hospital as she pleases. She's telling the truth when she says, "Nobody's forcing me to stay, Serrano; I'm only here to rest. I'm so tired. I feel like I've given birth to a walrus...to the whole herd."

She's become part of the scenery at the hospital. Lately she's spent more time here than anyplace else, four stays in four years.

The first time was to get out of going to jail after a conviction for reckless endangerment and defacing public property. After a wild night out she crashed into two cars and ran her own car into a palm tree in the traffic circle on Avenida Reforma. At the time of arrest she was in a state of euphoric delirium, a disorder whose most striking symptom is speech accelerated to the extreme that specialists call *taquipsiquia*, or the chatter of a motor-mouthed parrot. My experience with Liliana's *taquipsiquia* tells me it's set off by cocaine. I become its beneficiary on a night when she launches into a warp-speed description of the nasty things she wants to do to my body while she does them.

The prosecutor concedes that insane derangement is a mitigating factor and agrees to a sentence of involuntary confinement to a mental institution instead of jail. Upon her release the charges against Liliana will be dropped by the court. However, they will not be expunged from her police record pending successful completion of a period of conditional release in the custody of her sister Dorotea.

Once her case is resolved, Liliana remains on medication, and her doctors are reluctant to let her spend too much time away from the hospital. The stimulation of long periods in the outside world weakens her self-discipline. Sooner rather than later she stops taking her medications and tries to keep pace with the people around her. Trying to keep up with other people unhinges her. Her faltering ability to control herself becomes life-threatening and lands her back in the hospital. Her most recent readmissions were carried out with Liliana in so-called "soft restraints." She was placed in them by a star member of the Miranda Hospital psychiatric team, a compact woman with Asian eyes and a steely grip. Patients admitted under her auspices include: disobedient adolescents who threaten their parents with knives; young adults who perch on building ledges and beg for someone to listen to them before they kill themselves; and elderly invalids about to take a final dose of barbiturates provided by a sympathetic doctor. This small woman has twice come to Dorotea's house to place Liliana in soft restraints: once after she spent hours in the stable next to the house talking to her nephew's horse, Perleman; and once when Liliana drank too much and started ripping pages out of books in the studio of Dorotea's husband, Arno Heiser. After this second episode Dorotea visits Liliana in the hospital but refuses to invite her back into her house.

All this is explained to me by Dr. Barranco, a fortyish psychiatrist. Dr. Barranco is athletic and Caucasian. He has a salt-and-pepper beard which he styles with surgical precision. He has black eyes, a finely chiseled nose, and thick fingers with spatulate nails regularly cared for by a manicurist. While Dr. Barranco is speaking to me, I'm suddenly infuriated by the conviction that during one of their sessions he's had sex with Liliana. From my look or my silence Barranco must catch my drift because he suddenly trips on his tongue and loses his train of thought. Pompous medical terms cease to tumble so glibly from his soft pink lips. They're narrow lips that expose his white teeth and pink tongue when they part. I can easily picture that tongue and those lips probing Liliana's white and even teeth. I imagine them both with fangs bared to the world.

The main obstacle to Liliana's leaving the hospital is she has no money. By my calculations she's frittered away a fortune. By hers, just the equivalent of a couple of apartments she no longer owns. What really keeps her hospitalized is that she has nothing to live on day to day. The German pharmaceutical house run by Dorotea's husband covers Liliana's very considerable expenses as an inpatient. Dorotea could afford to keep her out and on her own for half as much. But Dorotea knows perfectly well that sooner or later her sister would run amok, and it would cost Dorotea dearly when she did.

At first I don't get what Liliana is asking for when she whispers in my ear, "Get me out of here." She wants to move in with me and have me support her. I'm deaf to the implications of her request and captivated by the warmth of her breath in my ear, the way her voice deepens when she whispers, "Get me out of here." She has me. The thought that a wish I've clung to forever might actually come true floods my whole body, my dream of Liliana Montoya. Not the Liliana of today or any other day but the Liliana of my dreams past, present, and future.

Sunday I make sure my visit coincides with Dorotea's so I can tell her I'm taking Liliana out of the hospital. I tell her I plan to live with Liliana.

After a long silence Dorotea replies.

"I disagree."

She warns Liliana, "You'll blow it."

She tells me, "You'll be sorry, Serrano."

The chill in her voice and her hypnotic glare frighten me. Strangely, the notion that I can spy on her, that I've spied on her already dispels my fright. Malaquías can rummage through every shred of her life and tell me all about it. In fact, Malaquías left me a disc with photos and videos from one of the days when he tracked Dorotea. I have so far chosen not to look at it. Remembering I have the disk bolsters the feeling of superiority gained from having spied on her. I need that superiority now.

My notebooks log the day I get Liliana out of the hospital, Thursday, September 25th, 2000. We have decided to live together in my house. Our first conjugal agreement is that she can rearrange the place any way she pleases, and I'll pay for it. I live in the same building in the Del Valle district of Mexico City where I've spent my whole life since marrying Aurelia Aburto, my Medusa. I still have the same apartment, but I own it now. I also bought the apartment next door. I took out a wall and turned the combined space into a large studio with books, paintings, and my two imperial desks. A critic said my studio and my desks have more claim to greatness than my writing. He may be right about that, but he's wrong about everything else.

Liliana's first question upon being shown around her new home is quite touching. She struggles to put her thoughts in order the way children sometimes do, and her eyes mist over when she looks at me:

"What would you like me to do, Serrano? I want to make you happy."

The days that follow are very strange, one routinely conjugal day after another except we never really connect. I don't know how to live with another person. It surprises me to come upon Liliana wandering around the apartment or sitting like a ghost in the sala. She spends hours listening to and organizing her tapes. She plans to put her songs on disc. She wears huge headphones so she can listen to her music without flooding the apartment with sound. Her ambulatory silence heightens the unreality of her presence. I know she's on the other side of the house while I'm writing. Sometimes I hear her come and go, but she seems to be somewhere else, in the world of her own voice and thoughts. Eerily silent.

She refuses to go out for fear of being led into temptation. A restaurant can be a gateway to hell. She consoles herself and me by cooking three meals a day:

breakfast, lunch, and a light dinner. Her ravenous appetite of times past is gone, and eating with her now is like being on a diet. Her meals consist of greens, watery soups, and unsweetened soft drinks. She tells me one day that she's been to see the the priest whose parish embraces our block. She's asked him if it's possible to believe in nothing. The priest replies that it can't be done because faith is synonymous with life itself. That's not true for her, she insists. The priest says he doesn't believe her. Liliana gives him a brief but truculent version of her life, which makes her feel better. I ask her to tell me what she told the priest:

"That's not for you to know, Serrano. It's for priests only."

She can't bear the thought of telling me what she told the priest. She puts her hands over her mouth, then goes on with a mix of amusement and horror.

"I'm a nun, Serrano. Does it make me a stranger to you? What would my father have said?"

She'd have been a stranger to the Jacobin Dr. Montoya too.

This is the first time I've ever heard her speak of her father, and I pass it off as a side effect of the pills. "Between pain and the abyss, pills," the old man might have said.

What happens next is she undresses, positions herself on her back, wriggles, pants, wraps her arms and legs around me, and closes her eyes. This is what I see from on top of her; her eyes are shut. She's not aroused, she doesn't stare at the ceiling while waiting for me to finish. She's turned in on herself, trying to see if she feels anything. Not like a working professional but like an accomplice going along with the request of a partner. She wants her partner to thrust. His love excites her, she'd like to reciprocate, but the best she can give back is this amatory placebo, neither rejection nor acceptance. The partner has earned the surrender of her body even though its hormones and heart have gone missing.

The pills.

Liliana is a medicated angel, a beautiful woman unmoved by desire. Beautiful but neuter. Her body has lost the tingle that flared at the least hint of intimacy, a look, a touch, wisps of underarm hair or the sole of a naked foot reflected in the tiles of a polished floor; now nothing can clear the path to a satisfying roll in the hay.

The first phase of our life together floats by like a cloud. Like an anodyne fog to be specific. The whole world is calm, clean, and hygienic. There are no rough edges, and it's all suffused in a dim shadowless light.

There's just one exception: the pills have left her voice intact. It's as hoarse and untamed as ever. I hear her singing in the shower. She's fond of "Paloma negra," a song that begins with a full-throated shriek of desperation:

> I'm tired of crying my
> sleepless nights away.
> I don't know if I should
> curse you or pray for you.

Liliana also begins at full voice as if she were performing outdoors in a rodeo ring. She's taking a shower in boiling hot water, and I can see her body through the glass door of the shower stall. I can see her body in the column of steam as she bathes and sings at the top of her lungs. I see she's not in distress, that the drops stream smooth and sparkling down her body, reddening the shade of her copper-hued skin. She rinses the first application of shampoo out of her hair. I watch her from the door to the bathroom, out of her sight. Her voice pierces the sealed glass door of the shower. When she comes to where the song says:

> I want to be free
> to live my life
> with the one I love.

she shudders and chokes as her voice drops to a low rumble, the protest of a wounded animal, possibly a pig with its throat slit.

This is how we are until the December morning when I wake up to find Liliana naked beside me. She's undressed and moist. The last night I remember her approaching me this way was in the dreary aftermath of our stay in Huitzilac a thousand years ago.

The morning is cold, but the gas heater keeps our bedroom warm. Rituals are rituals. Liliana stands with her back to the winter in the windows and bids me come hither. The spell cast by a gray day seen through fogged glass couldn't be more erotic. It's her first display of full frontal nudity since our time in Huitzilac came to an end. Her nakedness sets off in me a priapic firestorm unequalled in our years of shared nudity, years that are few in number and only rarely come near this summit of herculean grandeur; no adventure of the flesh ever surpasses the one about to begin the morning of Liliana's transformation. I'm not sure I mentioned that streaks of gray had begun to appear in the hair of her head and pubis.

"I quit the pills that don't let me want you, Serrano. Was that so bad?"

The doctor has said don't skip the pills. I know the pills induce apathy. I also know not taking them makes her hyper, and hyperactivity unchecked leads to the hospital. It's what scares me about Liliana, what's always scared me. But not this time. When she asks, "Was that so bad?" I tell her, "If that's bad, then let the bad times roll."

SHE'S NEVER BEEN AS BEAUTIFUL as in these days of madness. Never so mad as when she relapses into madness.

To be with her is to share her manic state. There comes a night when she can't fall asleep. She leaves at noon and doesn't come back. All I can do is wait for her. I wait in the worst possible way, sitting at my desk writing, pretending to read or write, on edge listening for the one sound I care about, the click of the lock in the door where she must enter. She reappears at noon. From my desk I hear the tumblers click in the lock. I do my best to look as if I'm writing.

"Stop your scribbling." She's standing in the doorway, remote, amused, knowing full well I've been waiting for her.

I don't answer, I don't move a muscle.

"No scribbling," she shouts in defiance of my silence.

"I told you no scribbling," she says for the third time as she plants herself before my desk.

She's brushed her hair into a coxcomb. There are slashes of black mascara on her eyelids. She laughs derisively at my silence and the way I look at her. She pirouettes.

"First I'll take a long bath, then I'll be ready for you."

She emerges from the bathroom wrapped in towels. She has the scrubbed face of a little girl.

"Nothing happened, Serrano. Do you want me to tell you about it, or will you offer me a drink?"

I offer her a drink. My house is full of possibilities. The wine cabinet is replenished daily under an unspoken agreement that it should never be empty. Bottles of tequila, whisky, local rum, and, inevitably, Liliana's vodka serve as ornaments on the dining room shelves pending consumption.

She's barefoot, damp, and browner than ever in her wrapping of white towels.

"I'm hungry, Serrano. Could you take me to eat at La Cantera?"

Her question refers to *La Casa de la Cantera*, or The Quarry House, a restaurant that serves Mexican food on Yucatán Street in the Roma district. It features trios whose songs entertain secretaries and their bosses in the steamy atmosphere of couples about to shut themselves up in hotel rooms for the balance of the evening. True to its name, La Cantera's pink walls are tumbled marble. Inlays in the floors and walls bespeak the caprices of designers steeped in tradition. I know what Liliana's going to say the minute we walk in the door. "The poet, journalist, and womanizer Renato Leduc had a table here. Tell the headwaiter we want Renato's table."

I slip the headwaiter a bill of an appropriate denomination and ask for Renato's table. He seats us in a comfortable corner of the large restaurant.

"For a start, you can recite *The Syphilitic Prometheus* for me," Liliana says after we sit down. It's the Leduc poem we've shared ever since her brother Rubén read it to us a thousand years ago, an ode to the language and the whores of his time. In the poem Leduc suggests that the gods made Prometheus's entrails rot with gonorrhea for teaching mortals they could fornicate in forty-six different positions, not just one.

"Tell it to me, Serrano. You taught it to me. 'Miserable mortals beating the bush for women.' Go ahead, Serrano, say it. 'Who copulate like iguanodons.' Go on, Serrano, you taught it to me."

I remind her that Rubén taught it to the two of us.

"Who can remember Rubén, Serrano? Who wants to talk about him? Do you want me to dry up thinking of Rubén? You taught me about Leduc, Serrano. At this table which was always reserved for him. I confess that one day I tried to take him home with me from another restaurant. I think it was called *El rincón de Cúchares*. He was around ninety, a few years before he died. I said, 'I'll support you, Renato. I'll dress you and take care of you and you'll die in my arms.' But he was very blind by then, and very old, though he was a very handsome old man. At his age he deserved to be pampered. You resemble Leduc, Serrano, you're a lot like him. Recite the other one you said was Leduc, the one about the smoke and the wind. I've always liked the way you recite, Serrano. I've always liked you, damn it. Even more now that we're together. I don't want to hold back, don't inhibit me. How did it go? 'If smoke stood still, if the wind came back.' Come on, Serrano: 'If you were to become yourself again.' You're back to being what you never were with me, Serrano. What'll we have to drink?"

I double our drink order. While it's being prepared I remember the dry and withered palm that grew in front of La Cava in better days, when it was a topflight restaurant. The first time I went to La Cava with

Liliana I stepped aside while she paid the bill with money from el *Pato* Vértiz. She'd just started going out with el *Pato*, and she was swimming in cash and credit cards as I think I mentioned already. She invited me for a meal the way people do when they get their first paycheck. "You don't want to know what el *Pato* does to me or what I do to him," she says. "Writers like you don't need to know about those things. They're supposed to use their imaginations." I can hear her hoarse voice saying, "I'm on my way up, Serranito. I'll see you in heaven."

Later, as we're leaving La Cava, she says, "When the time comes to break up with el *Pato*, you and I can eat here on my bill, this is where you and I will get together, Serrano. We'll live out the fate that's written in the palms of our hands. You and I will be meant for each other." In those days she also liked me to recite some lines from García Lorca that I'd memorized along with the ones from Leduc.

The ones from Lorca were:

Roosters seek the dawn
with their beaks as
Soledad Montoya comes down
from her dark mountain.

When I'd recite these lines, I'd put Liliana's name in place of Soledad's. She'd get excited and ask: "Which dark mountain is that, Serrano?" And I'd say, "Yours, of course."

Night is falling when we leave La Casa de la Cantera.

"I feel like singing, Serrano. What shall I sing for you? Will you take me to a bar I know?"

She takes me to the bar in the Hotel Amberes

where a piano player named Antonio greets her like a visiting diva. Liliana orders a bottle and sings three songs. Her voice is smooth and deep. When it drops into its lower register her mouth takes the shape of a kiss, and her bright red lipstick glows in the twilight of the bar. Standing next to the piano, microphone in hand, she dedicates her last song to me. It's called "The Lie." She approaches our table and sings in my face with her lips and eyes ablaze:

> *You keep forgetting*
> *that you love me*
> *despite what you say.*

Some idiot comes up to invite us for a drink and request a song. I tell him she's not a jukebox. Liliana smiles and is flattered.

"You've only stood up for me this once, and that's enough for me, Serrano. Pay no attention."

The piano player comes to our table after his set. His brilliantined hair is gray at the temples; he has the salt-and-pepper mustache of a crooner in times long past.

"You should make a record, *señora*," he tells Liliana. "A voice like yours shouldn't go unrecorded."

He hums with a voice ravaged by cigarettes.

> *You keep forgetting*
> *I can even do you*
> *harm if I want to.*

The piano player says: "You must make up your mind, *señora*."

"I already have, Antonio. Right now it's this gentleman." And by "this gentleman" she means me.

The character who wants Liliana to sing him a song is back at our table. Antonio the piano player gets up and herds him to his table. The recidivist glowers accusingly at me and points his finger. He's wearing a blue shirt with a tight collar and a red tie. He has an abundant head of straw-colored hair disheveled by drink.

"Dance?" Liliana says when we leave the Amberes.

We go back to the Roma district and a place called El Gran León, not far from La Casa de la Cantera where we'd been at midday. El Gran León is an expanded and more genteel version of the old Bar del León where we went on Brazil Street in the center of the city when we were young. A recycled combo from years past still plays there, Pepe Arévalo and His Mulattos. We're given a table by the dance floor and are swept backwards in time. The music is louder, the lights more blinding, our trip into memory more strident. Liliana has the bottle we didn't finish at Amberes in her handbag, but it doesn't keep her from ordering another one. No sooner is it served than a group comes in and takes over the table next to ours. The jerk who requested songs at the Amberes is in the group. He's more drunk than we are and taller than I am. His red necktie is still around the neck of his blue shirt, but the state of his straw-colored hair is worse than ever.

"You're the bastard from the other place," he says before sitting down at the next table. "And she's the one who refused to sing for her fans. You get my point, motherfucker? You do, don't you?"

Liliana calls the waiter and says something in his ear. In mine she says that when she goes to the restroom, I should get up and leave; she'll be waiting for me outside. Liliana gets up, and the creep with the red tie says, "Now will you sing for me?" He gets out a cigar, lights it, and stares at Liliana. He inhales and the ember grows.

"When I'm back from the ladies' room," Liliana says.

I wait for her to make her move, then head for the door. "I want to take you to my den," Liliana says when we're outside.

She directs the taxi driver across Reforma. We leave the Roma district and proceed to River Rhine in the Cuauhtémoc district where all the streets are named for rivers. The taxi stops in front of a stone mansion with Spanish grillwork and an enormous garage that's been converted into a sumptuous foyer leading into the three-story building. The place is called Olympus, a club for couples seeking couples. In dark rooms of varying sizes couples mingle according to their preferences: quartets, sextets, and symphony orchestras. There's a bar where patrons can make whatever arrangements they choose or do no more than drink. From the back of the kitchen—now become the manager's office and the storeroom for alcohol and stimulants—there emerges the ancient pusher from the old Cingaros, the immutable and shocking Minerva with the same lion's mane of hair. But in place of the bangs that once drew a sharp line across his wide forehead, he now sports a spiky efflorescence like a black hydrangea atop his ramrod straight stem of a body.

"Your room?" Minerva asks.

"My room," Liliana says.

"Provisions?" Minerva asks.

"To wake us up first and mellow us out

afterwards," Liliana instructs.

It all sounds ridiculous and mysterious to me.

Minerva escorts us to a room on the upper level, an addition built on top of the old roof. Wall-to-wall mattresses cover the floor. Water mattresses. There's just one window and no curtains in our room. Tonight the window lets the moonlight in.

While Minerva fetches the provisions, Liliana undresses herself, undresses me, and spreads the folded eiderdown on the bed over the two of us. It's light and smooth, large enough to wrap around us several times and envelope us like a silken sea.

Minerva brings Liliana her vodka in a miniature steel bottle in an ice bucket. He also brings a pillbox of lapis lazuli with a gram of cocaine and some pills I don't recognize. Liliana hurriedly opens the packet of cocaine and spills part of the powder on the eiderdown. She locates the spill with her nose and begins to inhale it first through one nostril, then the other. She collects what's left over with her fingers and rubs it into my nose, then she puts her fingers in my mouth and massages my gums. While doing this she takes deep gasping breaths as if on the verge of orgasm.

"You never take care of yourself, Serrano, so I'll take care of you." She goes on nonstop. About us, about old times. And about el *Catracho*. Rituals are rituals:

"Did I ever tell you I had someone killed, Serrano?"

We're finally back to where we ought to be, where we've always been.

I remind her she's already told me about it three

times.

"Three times?"

Three different times that don't match up, I tell her. I checked the date of execution, and it was wrong too.

"Wrong? Which date was wrong, Serrano?" The date she gave me for when it happened was wrong, I tell her.

"And what date did I give you, Serrano?"

I tell her Valentine's Day of 1978.

"Of 1978 no, Serrano. It was 1979. The 14th of February, 1979, silly."

I tell her I made that correction already. I found the error in the course of my investigation.

"Investigation, Serrano? You investigated what I told you? Why?"

To find out, I tell her.

"To find out, my ass, Serrano. Why? To turn the story of my life into a novel, you bastard? Isn't living it good enough? You haven't learned a thing. Let me tell you something. Do whatever you want, but don't come to me with the shit you investigated. What are you investigating for? Ask me anything, and I'll tell you the whole story. Not like your witnesses to the Huitzilac Massacre, who don't know a damn thing. I'll tell you one thing, Serrano, you poke around dead bodies like a vulture, you bastard. It makes no difference, go ahead and ask. But first tell me one thing. Do you really think I'd fuck up the way you say I did, or do you think I'm just a gossipy bitch?"

Both, I tell her.

"Both at once, Serrano?"

I tell her first one and then the other.

"So first I did it, and then I embroidered it, right, Serrano?" I nod, and she explodes.

"You bastard, you really think I could do it, don't you? And throw in extra seasoning to spice it up afterwards?"

I agree with that too.

"And that's why you're so afraid of me? Have you always been afraid of me?"

I nod twice.

"And that's the reason you never loved me, motherfucker?" I tell her I never loved anyone the way I love her.

"But without the balls to do anything about it," she says reproachfully. I admit it, without balls enough.

"At least you've got the balls to tell the truth. But what good does that do us now?"

I tell her it lets me be hers just the way I am. Right now she's got me with an erection worthy of a fifteen-year-old, the kind you only get in your sleep at my age.

She pushes the covers back and smiles:

"What are you thinking of, Serrano?"

She extends her hand to attend to me while we talk because what she wants right now is to talk. "Do you want to know what really happened, Serrano? You think I'm capable of everything I told you about because you're very gullible or very conceited, I don't know which. How can I explain it to you? I couldn't bring myself to do it, Serrano, but I did it. You know who made me do it? Dorotea. Do you believe me when I say it was Dorotea? She wouldn't leave me in peace until I told el *Pato* that el *Catracho* had to be killed or else. She kept after me until el *Pato* got it done. And then I didn't tell you. It was Dorotea all along, Serrano. Do you believe me now?"

She's very drunk, and so am I. Rituals are rituals.

"You wanted him killed, but he wasn't killed on orders from you," I tell her. "He was killed by mistake. Then el *Pato* was shown a body. He was told it was the man you were after, and that's what el *Pato* told you."

Her eagerness to talk keeps her from listening to what I tell her. Her monologue is all-consuming, and nothing matters except the urgency of her need to be believed.

"This is something I want to confess to you, Serrano. I'm not the one who had him killed. It wasn't my idea. It was Dorotea's. Day in, day out it was Dorotea who made me nag el *Pato* until he got it done. You see? And the one who insisted we had to see his dead body was Dorotea. My little sister Dorotea. You see? Then there was the lawsuit over el *Catracho*'s body, his relatives wanted it. El *Pato*'s friend the prosecutor asked el *Pato* to explain. El *Pato* made up a story. He said a top university official whose name he refused to reveal had asked for the execution. He said the top official was offended because Clotaldo dishonored his daughter."

This is the first time she uses el *Catracho*'s name. Clotaldo is one of the names I read in the press. She says it with a familiarity that hints at a layer to this story that hasn't been breeched yet. She forges ahead undeterred.

"The top official el *Pato* is talking about was me. El *Pato* covered up for me the same way I covered up for Dorotea. El *Pato*'s friend the prosecutor buried the file, but they got it out again when el *Pato* was running for the legislature. A lifelong friend and protégé threatened to give the file and everything else to the press. Does this sound familiar, Serrano? Do you know anything about this? Do you believe a single word of what I'm telling you? Order me another small bottle of vodka, will you? Just press this remote button. I'm taking what's left of the cocaine to the bathroom."

When she returns from the bathroom, I say and repeat at the peak of our inebriation, "You ordered the killing of el *Catracho*, but that's not why he was killed, he was killed by mistake. Then el *Pato* was told it was the body of the man he wanted killed, and el *Pato* told you."

"What are you talking about, Serrano? Stop playing the novelist. Come on and kiss me. Kiss me, and see what you get in return."

Dawn is coming in our window when we vacate the room. Passing through the vestibule on Liliana's arm, I'm knocked down. From the floor I see the creep in the blue shirt and red tie urging me to stand up and fight. His straw-colored hair is now a thicket sprouting unchecked from the top of his head.

The last thing I remember is that the scumbag is on top of me brandishing a jackknife, Liliana steps between us, I have a napkin over my arm and in my hand a bottle I intend to hit him with. Our scuffle attracts a swarm of shouting and jostling onlookers.

WHEN I OPEN MY EYES, I see el *Pato* Vértiz looking at me.

I'm sure it's a nightmare at first, but I'm not asleep. I'm in the hospital, and el *Pato* Vértiz is sitting in a chair at my bedside waiting for me to wake up. Behind him I can see Liliana. Her hangover has left her with immense bags under her eyes and hair in desperate need of a brush. She's listening to *Felo* Fernández who's talking a blue streak though no one is laughing. This unnerves me because normally when *Felo* Fernández talks, his listeners laugh. I revert to thinking it's either a nightmare or the fabled first step into the beyond. According to one expert, what the recently deceased see first are contorted images of the people who figured most prominently in the final moments of their lives.

Liliana hurries to embrace me when I wake up. Her embrace is effusive, but it feels as if she'd run me through with a sword. I'm told that my pain actually is attributable to a stab wound which a surgeon widened in order to rinse out my intestines and sew them back together. Liliana cries with the theatricality of a woman weeping in church. I don't recall ever seeing her cry so wholeheartedly before. Grief ill becomes her; it disfigures her face and makes her hoarse. El *Pato* says he's here to tell me what happened. I tell him he wasn't there when whatever happened happened. I ask what happened. Liliana explains that the creep who followed us from the bar at the Hotel Amberes to the Olympus got me with his jackknife. The trusty Minerva stopped him as he was about to slit my throat. Liliana also piled on top of him. As in the words of many a crime story, the perpetrator got away.

I have a five-inch wound below my navel where the blade slashed me and the doctor operated. I've been unconscious for a whole day with a high fever and a stubborn infection. I'm totally screwed over, but what is el *Pato* Vértiz doing in the hospital room where I'm lying on my deathbed? I'm too weak to ask. My efforts to speak are stifled by the pain in my stomach that cries out: "Don't talk, asshole." But I want to speak, to ask, for instance, who told el *Pato* Vértiz to come here. *Felo* Fernández is fine, but el *Pato*? Forget it! All I need now is for Dorotea and her genius son or Dr. Barranco to show up.

With all the sarcasm I can muster I ask why no one has called Dr. Barranco. Liliana answers with no trace of sarcasm that she called him, but he's out of town. Now more than ever I'm convinced that Barranco has been screwing Liliana during her therapy sessions. I ask if I can be put back to sleep. I'm told the doctor's orders are for me to get out of bed and walk when I wake up. "Fuck walking," I reply as Dorotea appears in the doorway as if by magic. I don't recall ever seeing her so beautiful, tan and pale with the pensive gaze of the Virgin of Guadalupe. Bathed in light, she glides from the doorway to my sickbed. My hospital room is quite large, to be sure. There's an operable picture window, a small side room and space enough for Dorotea to seem to levitate as she approaches my bed. I wonder about the cost of this room where

Dorotea walks in as if on air and that someone has to pay for. I think I'll ask Dorotea's husband for a loan. Does the husband have a clue about the woman who lives within Dorotea?

I know I'm delirious because my hypothesis of moments ago is back: I must be at the early postmortem phase when the experts say the dead begin their fabled trip into the beyond. We take our first step on this journey while standing at death's door and watching our lives pass before our eyes. In the grip of this dreary suspicion I'm miffed by the thought that those gathered around me as I depart this life are two museum-quality sisters, the decrepit el *Pato*, the fornicating Dr. Barranco, and *Felo* Fernández, who should at least be able to come up with a joke that will get a laugh out of this disastrous assemblage.

Instead, *Felo* makes matters worse by whispering in my ear that el *Pato* has an idea or a possible explanation for what has happened. What has happened isn't mere coincidence, *Felo* says, but the start of something el *Pato* is very clear about. I don't know how this scene of the fabled first step dissipates or what makes my grotesque premonitions of rust and rot vanish. But when I emerge from my hallucinations, I feel refreshed and unburdened, I might even say lucid although it's a word that's never felt right to me. There are things in life that I've been able to see clearly, but I don't see them lucidly. With the possible exception of Liliana's lambent flesh and, now that I'm fully awake, the memory of Dorotea gliding across my hospital room.

I come to. The hospital room I'm in is pure shit, small, dark, and drab. It's nighttime, and the feeble glow of those little lights the overnight nurses and doctors leave on is all the light there is, a crumb of luminosity that can be found in shitty hospital rooms the world over.

My lips are dry, my neck is aflame, and my eyes are swollen as well as dry. My eyelids feel as if they're being held open by pliers while some toxic liquid swims about my eyeballs. If I'm not dead, I wish I were. In this gloom that mimics death I see that, fortunately, I'm in a single room. Liliana sleeps in the recliner next to my bed. But she isn't sleeping. She is leaning back with her eyes open, staring at the ceiling. She doesn't know I'm awake. She may be praying. I ask her if she's praying. At the sound of my voice she sits up and says, no, she's not praying. I ask if everybody has left. She asks what do I mean by everybody. I tell her el *Pato*, *Felo*, Dr. Barranco, and Dorotea. I ask if el *Catracho* happened by.

"You're delirious," she says. "You're still delirious. And I was, too."

I ask her to tell me about her delirium.

"What ails me isn't delirium, Serrano. It's reality." I ask her which reality is that.

"I destroy everything I touch." I ask what everything she touches includes.

"Everything, Serrano. Look at yourself. And el *Pato*, and Rubén, and Dorotea. Look at what Dorotea's stuck with."

She seems convinced that Dorotea played a part in my hospitalization. I don't have to prompt her to say why. "I'm haunted by all the bad things I did, Serrano. They keep coming back, and they don't go away. You're the only good thing that comes back.

And look at you, lying there with your gut cut open by a jerk with the hots for me. All I want is to die, Serrano."

I tell her she has to get me out of the hospital first. She laughs, but judging by her look, it's not a real laugh. We've hit another dead end, but I don't let it bother me right now. I'm intrigued by what else she says about el *Pato*, Rubén, Dorotea. The ruin of el *Pato* is inconsequential, a rare accident of existential justice. That's not the case with Rubén, much less Dorotea. I know Rubén has become a cranky alcoholic whose career has gone nowhere, but I didn't know Liliana played a part in his downfall. I ask her how Rubén came to grief.

"I turned him down, Serrano. I always said no, but he never stopped asking. One day he tried to poison himself with Nembutal. He didn't die, but it made him the failure he's become."

I sense a gap in her answer. I ask her to explain, and she does. She says Rubén needed her to love him. That's exactly how she says it: "He needed me to love him." I sense with blinding clarity that she's lying while also telling the truth.

I ask if she met his need.

"Never."

I ask if she let Rubén inside her.

She stares at the ceiling. I ask her again if she ever let Rubén inside her.

"Once."

Her shared confidence arouses me.

"Three days one Holy Week," Liliana says. "Those three days and never again, Serrano."

I also remember coming on to her during a Holy

Week. Her mother customarily spent Holy Week in Morelia. I ask if I was Rubén's replacement.

"He went crazy when he found out about you."

I repeat, "Was I Rubén's replacement?"

"You were always you, Serrano. At first you and Rubén were both on my mind. But not later. When Rubén found out about you, he went mad. But I never let him inside me again. It made him crazy when I let him and then when I didn't let him. I don't know what I'm talking about. I'm lost. This hospital makes me sick. Nothing makes sense here, nothing seems true." I ask her what other revelations she has for me now that she's told me everything. I ask if we've finally come to the threshold of Dorotea's secret doorway.

"Dorotea is my permanent secret, Serrano." I ask her to tell me that secret.

"I already did, Serrano. What happened today was all because of Dorotea. Dorotea is like a seer. She's done whatever was necessary to make things turn out the way she wanted. My sister makes me insane, Serrano. She's always making me crazy."

Liliana continues unprompted.

"Can I tell you the truth? Dorotea adored el *Catracho*. He was her grown-up boyfriend, her sugar daddy. Like el *Pato* was for me. Dorotea adored him."

I remind her that el *Pato* is a sore subject between us.

"El *Catracho* adored Dorotea, too, Serrano. He didn't dishonor her, he adored her."

I ask why Dorotea hated el *Catracho*.

"Because Dorotea is Dorotea, Serrano. Because el *Catracho* cheated on her, and she wouldn't forgive him."

I ask her why she feels responsible for el *Catracho* and Dorotea.

"Because I had him killed, Serrano, don't be stupid. I had him killed. And I took her to her first parties with older people. I wanted her to get to know how the world works at an early age. And I took her to the party where she met Clotaldo. Because of me she met Clotaldo and fell for him heart and soul. Then one day she snubbed him, and Clotaldo retaliated by making sure she saw him with another girl. Dorotea wasn't about to forgive him for that. She told el *Pato* and me that Clotaldo treated her like a whore and humiliated her. She made a big deal out of it and told me she was going to kill herself. She had no intention of killing herself. But I told el *Pato* to get rid of el *Catracho*. You know the rest of the story, motherfucker, so don't be tormenting me with it."

I suppose the look on my face robs her story of its melodrama. I'm shattered to find Liliana's more swayed by melodrama than tragedy, and it makes my feelings for her feel more superficial, more shallow.

The hospital is driving me crazy.

I fall asleep and dream. Dorotea glides towards me. She whispers in my ear that she wants to do with me what Rubén did with Liliana. The figure of a young el *Catracho* hovers in the background unscathed by the bullets that ruined his face. And behind the youthful and unbloodied el *Catracho* is the desiccated countenance of Comandante Neri in foul conversation with el *Pato* Vértiz. The summer is hellishly hot, then a breath of cool air blows in from the sea or maybe from a fan that someone pointed at our neck to refresh our memories.

I realize I'm still hallucinating. I don't know how much of what I remember actually happens in the real world and how much is the mad imaginings of my dream. I do know I wake up with certainties I didn't have before I went to sleep, the worst of them being the knowledge that, just as I'd done, Rubén penetrated Liliana during Holy week.

I leave the hospital with Dorotea imprinted on my forehead.

THE NIGHTMARE ABOUT el *Pato* Vértiz that I had in the hospital comes true when I get out. I convalesce at home for two weeks. Liliana's been on the pills that stabilize her mood for two weeks. She takes on the role of nurse with quiet grace or as a step towards grace. She looks after me with the solicitude and submissiveness of a nun, assuming that, as my caregiver, she is otherwise lost to me and to herself. To both of us.

One afternoon as the sinking sun warms the windows, *Felo* Fernández brings el *Pato* Vértiz to my studio. He does it with Liliana's consent, and, says *Felo*, el *Pato* wishes to trust me with a secret. It's up to me to listen and decide. I have a soft spot for *Felo* Fernández not unlike the one he has for el *Pato* Vértiz. I resign myself to what sounds like a done deal. El *Pato* has come to my studio with a bundle of papers held up by his right arm and supported—though just barely—on his hip. Liliana leaves the studio with her customary circumspection and, I suspect, by prior agreement with *Felo*. Unaware of her departure, *Felo* holds his piece a moment more. Liliana reappears at the door and motions with her finger for him to leave too.

I'm left alone with el *Pato* Vértiz, his freckled bald spot, his misshapen nose, his obscene gut, his lips discolored by asthma or emphysema. El *Pato* places his bundle on the table in the small parlor between my imperial desks and prepares to tell me what he wants. I interrupt before he can say a word: I'll listen to what he has to say provided he agrees to tell me everything he knows about el *Catracho* and Dorotea. The way he burrows down in his chair testifies to the fear he must be living with. The conversation that follows is meaningless to me personally although el *Pato* does say some interesting things that merit inclusion in this story.

El *Pato* says the papers he's laid on the table summarize his investigation of his former protégé, Ricardo Antúnez. He's not avoiding my question about Dorotea and el *Catracho*, he stresses, nor does he intend to. He's spent years gathering proof of crimes committed by the police during the period when el *Catracho* was murdered. According to him, everything going on now, including my current convalescence, has roots in the distant past. It's all part of Antúnez's quest for vengeance, he states.

I ask why Antúnez is worried about police behavior in the 1970s when he was just a beginning functionary in the law-enforcement bureaucracy. El *Pato* says his investigation proves Antúnez was, and still is, a staunch proponent of what the police once called "social hygiene." The term refers to the way cases of slander or violence were sometimes resolved in the past. At the request of the alleged victim, old-school policemen would liquidate the alleged perpetrator. El *Pato* says he has proof that many cases were resolved in this fashion, including some recent ones that Antúnez closed by resorting to "social hygiene." What Antúnez does isn't merely a vestige of past misconduct; it's part of a criminal apparatus that has never been dismantled.

El *Pato* says he made the mistake of confiding his findings to Olivares, who half in jest and half in earnest mentioned them to Antúnez. To Olivares it was just a passing remark to an old friend who sold espionage services to the agency he headed, the place where he also found a spot for his old mentor el *Pato*. Antúnez reacted to what he heard by having Olivares put to death.

"Olivares died a few weeks after chatting with Antúnez," el *Pato* states, adding that his death serves as a grim warning to him.

I ask why Antúnez would want Olivares dead if he was only the messenger and not el *Pato*, who was the real threat. El *Pato* explains that he and Antúnez have watched each other warily for years, and Antúnez knows el *Pato* wouldn't be an easy kill. And knowing what Olivares told Antúnez, el *Pato* put his papers in a safe place and warned Antúnez that they would be made public if anything happened to him. So Antúnez took action against Olivares. The day after the wake el *Pato* let Antúnez know he got the message and agreed to his conditions for keeping silent. He did this through an obituary with a coded message that el *Pato* repeats to me word for word and which I strike from my notes as soon as I hear it.

We've reached the point where I come on the scene, according to el *Pato*. He says Antúnez is alarmed when he hears I asked *Felo* Fernández if he knows someone who can get me el *Catracho's* file. My request leaves him in the dark, so he goes to Antúnez. Antúnez imagines el *Pato* has broken their agreement and fears he's about to use me, the clueless writer, as the fuse to set off a scandal.

"You had your own reasons for asking about el *Catracho*," el *Pato* says. "But Antúnez felt that with Olivares out of the way, I was pitting you against him." I ask if he thinks I was knifed on orders from Antúnez, that the attack was meant as a warning. Without a doubt; in el *Pato*'s mind it all fits together.

It all fits together so implausibly that el *Pato* might not be making it up. He just might, as the saying goes, be telling it like it is. And it may sound worse than it is because el *Pato* tries hard to make his disclosures seem as ominous as possible. His digressions annoy me. His pauses and equivocations belong to a kind of public discourse that deliberately overlooks doubt while pretending to be sincere. There's no hiding the skepticism that must be written all over my face. I get out of this impasse by saying he still hasn't answered my question about Dorotea and el *Catracho*. El *Pato* retreats into his shell. I look him straight in the eye with an icy stare intended to stress that I can do without the circumlocutions. He gets the point and says:

"That night I was in the place where el *Catracho* died."

He looks up at the ceiling and wrings his hands.

"They took some pictures of me."

He runs his left hand over his bald spot, then his right hand.

"Later they used those photos to put the squeeze on me." He looks up at the ceiling then down at the floor. "To squeeze money out of me and the person with me."

I have a hunch that he has more to say but isn't sure he should say it. I ask who was with him and watch him squirm under the cold, unseeing stare that frightened him once already and threatens to turn homicidal if he says the wrong thing now.

He gets to his feet and rubs his shrunken buttocks with both hands; they slide easily under the loose trousers his body no longer fills.

"What I must tell you," he says at last, "is that the person with me wasn't Liliana."

I focus on him so hard he doesn't dare look away. He knows by my eyes that I'm ordering him to go on. He begins to sweat as if he'd been caught under the glare of a ceiling lamp hung just above his head.

"It was Dorotea."

My hunch has paid off. A rush of pleasure bursts up from my sweaty invalid's back and floods my chest. El *Pato* lets himself go. "Seeing Dorotea in that place would have made your hair stand on end, I can tell you that."

He paces the floor in front of me, caught up in the scene he describes.

"Dorotea took one look at el *Catracho*'s cadaver, and you can't imagine what she did. She turned his head with her foot so she could see the side of his face. Then she turned him so she could see his face full on. I'd seen Dorotea and el *Catracho* together. Liliana and I had gone out with them. I had seen that Dorotea loved el *Catracho* just as much as Liliana loved me. I'm not boasting, don't be offended, that's just the way it was. I don't know why these two incredible sisters fell for Clotaldo and me. Something must be wrong with the world for these things to happen, but they happen anyway. I've seen it everywhere. This kind of girl can't wait to see the world. What can I say? We loved them, and we used them. But they wanted us to use them. Don't be angry. Being abused excited them. They wanted to be worldly, to lose their virtue. And their loss was our gain."

He choked on this last remark. His cheeks reddened with emotion, and his eyes filled with tears.

I tell him to stow the comments and get back to the facts. He said el *Catracho* was killed at noon. Antúnez sent him the photos of el *Catracho*'s body that afternoon, and he took them to Liliana that night. Liliana showed them to Dorotea. Dorotea demanded to see the corpse. Antúnez ordered Neri to take them to the site of the killing. While they were looking at el *Catracho*'s body, Neri snapped two photos. Antúnez had them sent to el *Pato*, who destroyed them. Years later when Antúnez ran against him for a seat in the Mexico City legislature, Antúnez sent him copies of the photos and threatened to show them to the press and tell how they came to be taken unless el *Pato* withdrew. El *Pato* dropped out of the race.

That was his worst-ever mistake, he says. He let Antúnez see he was frightened. Antúnez won the election and went on to the political career that should have been el *Pato*'s. Given his dubious merits, Antúnez didn't last long in politics. After he left office, Neri once again approached el *Pato* with the photos he also had saved. He wanted money. El *Pato* paid him hush money for ten years without knowing if Neri was blackmailing him for his own personal benefit or for Antúnez. For a long time el *Pato* thought it would be just like Antúnez to remind him who was boss by putting the squeeze on him. He finally decided to seek his revenge by investigating the period when Antúnez was a minor player in the world of law enforcement. He meant to settle the score between them by practicing politics in a different way. Alerting the community about people like Antúnez, he says, is an act of political responsibility, and he discovered that Antúnez still practiced policing the old-fashioned way. For him, killing lawbreakers was "social hygiene."

His investigation isn't complete, el *Pato* says. The files, copies of which he's put on my table, wouldn't stand up in court. The misconduct they describe and the proof they offer doesn't track current codes and regulations neatly enough; charges based on existing law would be subject to challenge and likely be thrown out on legal technicalities. Which is why el *Pato* hasn't spoken out about his investigation. He's serious about what he's doing. He has no intention of releasing information that isn't actionable. He doesn't want to bring charges that look solid in the press but flimsy to a judge. He wants to sink Antúnez, not just discredit him.

He recites all this haltingly and gets bogged down trying to fend off doubts before I can raise them. The quality of his information may be sound, but I don't think he has the willpower to take it very far. He's crippled by fear. He's long since lost the sense of impunity and belief in his own innocence needed to press on in the face of adversity. He seems less eager to do battle with Antúnez than to find someone he can make a deal with. Now, as in the past, he doesn't know if he wants to fight or negotiate, and this uncertainty makes him unable to do either one.

I ask if Neri also took photos of el *Catracho* to Dorotea, if he tried to blackmail her too. As I say this, I realize that, at this stage of my convalescence, the only thoughts that stir my brain are about Dorotea.

"I don't know," el *Pato* says.

For the first and only time this afternoon I feel he's telling the truth. And that truth in effect tells me he doesn't know what I want to find out.

When *Felo* Fernández and Lilliana come into my studio with curious looks on their faces, it occurs to me that there's a fine but unbreakable line separating close relatives on one side from friends and lovers on the other. There's also a fine inner thread that separates each of us from ourselves by age: youth from when youth ends and from every change thereafter until the thin thread of life can no longer hold us together.

LILIANA TAKES CARE OF ME until I'm strong enough to bathe, walk around the house, and go out on the street unassisted. When my surgical wound is fully healed she takes me out on the town one last time. With her it's always the last time. At dawn we're in a room at the legendary Tlacoquemécatl Inn and very drunk. She lets me have her body for the rest of the morning, and I'm able to use it. I sleep all afternoon.

That night I find her sitting in our sala in the dark looking out the window. The yellow light of a street lamp illuminates half of her body and her face. I sit down next to the part of her that's in shadow.

"You have to let me go my own way, Serrano." I ask to where.

"To hell, Serrano. To hell."

One of her big dark eyes trembles as she speaks. For the first time in my life, or maybe just the first time I remember, she seems less alluring than fragile. She's the woman I've always loved, the one I can't stop loving, but all of a sudden she seems fragile, and in her fragility she seems less lovable, less irresistible. As with any married couple, there are things we must sort out. It's a process I know something about. What's different this time is Liliana's only wish is to leave, and I ask nothing in return for letting her go. But she has a plan. Do I want her to tell me about it?

She's reached an agreement with Dorotea. She'll

return to the hospital and go back on the pills. Under treatment she'll get used to living at odds with herself, and upon release from the hospital she'll move to Dorotea's house. Together they'll open a boutique hotel like the one Liliana managed for a few years in Antigua. Had she already told me about her hotel in Antigua? One night on a drunk she burnt it down, then she decided to mend her ways. She smiles wickedly. She won't set fire to another hotel. At first she'll live at Dorotea's, then she'll move into the hotel, just like in Antigua. She asks if I could live this way or would it remind me too much of my marriages.

I say her plan reminds me of my marriages. She hastens to say she doesn't want to marry me. She wants to be married to Dorotea and the hotel for the same reason I married the women I did: to be at peace with herself. She knows all marriages—including mine and hers to Dorotea—fall apart and the partners go back to war. The pills are just another way to rest and gather strength for the next battle. This, I suggest, evokes the metaphor of the winter barracks: two armies fight an endless war except in winter when each side returns to barracks. But that's exactly how she can get along with Dorotea, she insists. They'll live together as long as the pills keep the peace. When Liliana can't stand the pills anymore and quits taking them so she can be herself again, she'll leave Dorotea's house and promise not to return until the war is over. They both know the war will resume. When it does, Liliana must be strong enough to leave and come back or to leave and not come back. Dorotea has told her that if she wants to die, she'll have to die somewhere else, not at home with her and her son. This is the only condition

Dorotea imposes, and Liliana vows to respect it. She asks if I share Dorotea's condition. I say, no, I don't. When her peace with Dorotea breaks down, she asks, can she come and wage war with me?

I know the sisters consider me a pushover. It suits the purposes of their scheme, but it doesn't particularly hurt my feelings. I tell her she can come whenever she wants, preferably minus the pills. We seal our pact by crawling back into bed with a sadness that won't let us talk or sleep.

The big event of the following day is that Dorotea pays us a visit. She's come to get Liliana and readmit her to the hospital. I bristle at the thought of letting Dr. Barranco get his favorite patient back in his pen.

"I didn't mince words, Serrano. I told you you'd be sorry."

She speaks in a voice that's all edge as if she were going to burst out laughing. She's like an actress in a play, and, as she and I know full well, we've reached the moment when reality sets in and it's no use pretending otherwise She has the wide-set eyes of a comic strip belle; her long lashes turn up at the corners giving her a feline look that she accents with carefully applied underscores of eyeliner. The delicate flare of her nose is reminiscent of the Virgin in Renaissance portraiture. Her lips are thin but well formed. In repose they are shaped like the beginning or the end of a smile. The beautiful child she once was lives on in the alert, ironic and poised woman she's become.

Dorotea says, "Promise to come visit us, Serrano."

"I already made a deal with him," Liliana breaks in. "He'll be my cemetery of last resort."

"I wish someone would love me like that before I

die," Dorotea says. "Or would have loved me."

She kisses me on the cheek. Her lips are moist and cold. I feel the smoothness of her saliva.

Weeks go by. The day Liliana leaves the hospital to live at her sister's house, she phones me. She wants me to visit them, she has news from Rubén. She wants me to call on her whenever and however I please. She hasn't forgotten me. She and Dorotea are together and at peace.

What attracts me to the sisters isn't peace but war. Added to that is the intriguing way Dorotea has stepped out from behind the enormous and dominating shadow of Liliana.

The day I visit them the maid knows I'm coming. She lets me in and she says the ladies are expecting me in the garden. They're sitting under an umbrella at the wrought iron table with their backs to me, looking across the lawn to the woods and the stable. They're dressed in white; a light breeze ripples Liliana's hair without raising a single strand of Dorotea's. They chat peaceably and mysteriously. I pause to take in the scene before me and wonder how genuine can this aura of peace and serenity really be. Can I make their peace complete by repeating now what I'd told Liliana to no effect whatsoever? Namely: "The two of you didn't kill el *Catracho*. You gave orders to have him killed, but you didn't kill him. You wanted him to die, and you had the means to make him die, but, unlike your emotions, your means never came into play."

I don't know if what I have to say is true. All I have to go on is the version of Comandante Neri, and for me Neri lost much of his credibility by serving as Antúnez's willing accomplice. It now strikes me that the truth wouldn't change the answer to a question that has bedeviled me throughout my investigation. Is it possible that what's most important is not what actually happened but what the sisters think happened? They think Dorotea's boyfriend, el *Catracho* Clotaldo, was killed on orders from them. It's what Liliana told el *Pato* to do, and she still assumes el *Pato* got it done at her request. Dorotea went to see her lover's cadaver, and the sight of a body lying dead on the floor satisfied her that her wish had been granted. While he lived she was implacable; she claimed he prostituted and brutalized her when he'd only made her mad. She was even more hardhearted after he died. She demanded to see the body. To make sure the life had gone out of it, she moved the head back and forth with the toe of her shoe.

From day one the thought that the sisters got away with something has buzzed like a fly inside my head. Could these two women, who are legendary to me, cause the death of someone they loved and live the rest of their lives unburdened by remorse? The Montoya sisters sit with their backs to me in the garden behind Dorotea's house, and I can imagine them saying, yes, they could. The lives of these two women, at least their lives with me, are riddled with fallout from their crime. They are in their own way a separate species. Mythically, erotically, and irresistibly remote; arousing, dark and impenetrable up close.

Once greetings are exchanged, I ask if it's all right with them if I write up the story of el *Catracho*.

"Write what you like," Liliana says.

"Whatever you want," Dorotea says. "But who is this el *Catracho* person? What are you talking about anyway? You pestered me about that the last time you visited, and it made me dizzy. Some of the things you said were downright crazy, Serrano. Would you like some fresh cream? They brought some from the dairy barn today."

She says they came across the last dairy barn to survive in a corner of the city now invaded by enormous houses with elaborate country gardens. Dorotea didn't want the dairy barn shut down so her husband Arno got an organic restaurant to buy it, and the former owners stayed on as employees. They're very pleased with the deal and very grateful to Dorotea and her husband for helping to arrange it. They often send over raw milk, fresh cream, and whole-milk butter, a point Dorotea goes on about at length before saying:

"The last time you came I didn't show you my cactus garden, did I?"

Her last words are hardly out of her mouth before she is on her feet and walking towards the stable. To one side of the stable is the secret spot where Dorotea has her cactus garden. She tells me about it as we walk.

"Cacti aren't as popular as cypresses or jacarandas, Serrano, but they're truly the salt of the earth. They need very little water and no care at all. They're desert plants, they don't die because they don't wilt. They store moisture in their stalks. In very bad droughts they go dormant; they shrink, and their skins toughen up to keep the water inside them from evaporating. When it rains they don't get waterlogged, they absorb only what they need. They come in all shapes and sizes. Some have spines, but others don't. Cacti with no spines are called succulents. They can be tiny or gigantic. Desert saguaros can grow as high as sixty feet. There are succulents the size of a crystal ball that live for three hundred years. I'm a cactus, Serrano; Liliana's a jacaranda. They shed profusely every year and then dry up. The don't retain water. Jacarandas are very beautiful, to be sure, but cacti are the salt of the earth."

She begins to show me the cactus garden she planted around a pond not much bigger than a puddle, an exuberant collection of desert plants that thrive in small pots of arid soil: globe cacti, prickly pears, agaves, evergreens. She shows me a pot with four shoots as round and hairy as a penis, what she calls an old-man cactus due to its unruly headdress of white hair. One day she overwatered the old man, and it began to wither from being pampered. By the time she noticed, half the plant had rotted, and that taught her a lesson. She sliced the old man's four penises in half and threw the rotted sections in a bed of ashes, expecting they'd die. Neglect and lack of water brought the old man back from a bed of its own ashes.

"From that old man I learned what life is all about, Serrano. To stay healthy you must cut and prune."

She gives me an ironic and knowing look, a skeptical, slightly sleepy look through half-closed eyes.

We return in silence to where Liliana waits for us under the umbrella. Dorotea continues into the house leaving me alone with Liliana, who has not said a word. It would be a good time to talk. For her to tell me about Rubén, for me to tell her what my life is like without her. But I don't feel like talking with Liliana right now. I'd rather have my eyes on Dorotea. I watch her walk through the garden towards the house with its big picture window reflecting the woods behind me. I notice she's barefoot. Her pace is slow, upright and entrancing.

Oh, if I could only get my fill of watching Dorotea instead of Liliana. Dorotea is the woman I could look at with childlike innocence, like a brother looking at a sister and seeing the enigmatic body that opens the doors to the world.

AROUND THIS TIME Comandante Neri is in the news and in jail. Someone had the bright idea of naming him deputy chief of the Mexico City police. The appointment makes him a public figure, and the press discovers he has a fugitive son with a kidnapping charge pending against him. The resulting uproar forces Neri to resign the same day the story breaks. A short while later the police follow him to his son's hideout where officers rescue a doctor and his secretary who have been held captive for two months. I see Neri's familiar face in newscasts as he tells the cameras the trumped-up case against him and his son stems from an ancient squabble within the ranks of the police; his son was on the run from other trumped-up charges filed by enemies of his own. When asked to name his enemies he has the effrontery to accuse the chief of the federal police whose rivalry with the city police is longstanding. "My son was a fugitive for reasons of self-defense," Neri says. "I accepted my appointment thinking I could clear his name. It's all a mess, and look where it got me. That's the way it is with Mexican justice. You never know whose hands you're in."

His words sound sincere and fresh. Or perhaps just cynical and eloquent.

Antúnez isn't in any of the news stories. I call *Felo* Fernández to ask about him, and *Felo* tells me he's gone missing. His office says he's out of the country. I ask if he's a fugitive.

"For him that would be perfect, boss, because his next stop would be jail."

Liliana comes back to me twice under her agreement with Dorotea. On the first occasion I ended up under arrest in the hospital. On the second she lost the small finger of her left hand. I'm not telling how these outings got derailed, nor am I going to sensationalize them in an account already full of similar escapades. I remember very little about our adventures in that great happy mist where the true, timeless and brilliant treasures of my final days with Liliana Montoya lie buried.

There's not a moment's boredom in that mist. It's all time well spent though I can't remember any of it. It glows inside me, as real as a lost empire, a vanished civilization. What does remain is enough for me, the name of a bar, a dark hallway, sweat trickling down Liliana's naked back. There is nothing for me to proclaim with such limitless joy in the rest of my routine and unremarkable life.

About
HÉCTOR AGUILAR CAMÍN

HÉCTOR AGUILAR CAMÍN (born July 9, 1946 in Chetumal) is a Mexican writer, journalist and historian. As a journalist, he has written for *Unomásuno* and *La jornada*, the magazine *Proceso*, and currently for *Milenio*. He founded and is the editor of *Nexos*, one of the leading Mexican cultural magazines. In 2016 his memoir *Adiós a los padres* (due out from Schaffner Press in 2018) was shortlisted for the Vargas Llosa Prize. In 2017 he received a lifetime achievement award from Mexico's Instituto de Bellas Artes, the country's top cultural institution. *Day In, Day Out* is his second novel to be translated into English.

About
CHANDLER THOMPSON

In the 1960s Chandler Thompson was a Peace Corps Volunteer in Colombia, then a translator from French and Spanish to English for a wire service in Paris. He has been an interpreter for the U.S. State Department and the federal courts. He has covered Mexico as a stringer for *The Christian Science Monitor* and as a staff reporter for *The El Paso Times*. He began translating the novels of Héctor Aguilar Camín in 2006.